About the author

David has moved from New Jersey to California to Illinois to California to different parts of California to Colorado. With each new place, David brings new life to his writing. David devotes his time to his dog, his family, his friends, and his writing (in that order.) Mostly, David hopes his writing can bring a little illumination, sadness, or joy to someone or anyone.

PI Arlo and the Case of the Chocolate Cul-de-Sac

David Shannon Allen

PI Arlo and the Case of the Chocolate Cul-de-Sac

Pegasus

PEGASUS PAPERBACK

© Copyright 2025 **David Shannon Allen**

The right of David Shannon Allen to be identified as author of this work
has been asserted by him in accordance with the Copyright, Designs
and Patents Act 1988

All Rights Reserved

No reproduction, copy or transmission of this publication
may be made without written permission.
No paragraph of this publication may be reproduced,
copied or transmitted save with the written permission of the publisher,
or in accordance with the provisions
of the Copyright Act 1956 (as amended).

This is a work of fiction. Names, characters, businesses, places, events
and incidents are either the products of the author's imagination or used
in a fictitious manner. Any resemblance to actual persons, living or
dead, or actual events is purely coincidental.

Any person who does any unauthorised act in relation to this publication
may be liable to criminal prosecution and civil claims for damage.

A CIP catalogue record for this title is available from the British Library

ISBN-978-1-80468-086-5

Pegasus is an imprint of
Pegasus Elliot MacKenzie Publishers Ltd.
www.pegasuspublishers.com

First Published in 2025

Pegasus
Sheraton House Castle Park
Cambridge CB3 0AX England

Printed & Bound in Great Britain

Acknowledgments

Thank you to Skye without whom this would be a very different form of writing and would be gathering dust as a screenplay file on my computer.

Dedications

To my cantankerous pup, Arlo—the dog behind the
fictional dog.

Chapter 1
The 24-Hour News Cycle

The dimly lit hallway had a flickering light and a barren wasteland of mostly unoccupied apartments. The city was overcrowded, but that didn't make this place any more appealing to anyone. Overpriced and undermanaged, the hallway led all the way to a frosted glass-paned wooden doorway that read two simple words and represented two of the city's most underappreciated detectives: 'Arlonius Investigations.'

Behind the door, there was a wildly unprofessional living room. The head detective of Arlonius Investigations sat with his partner on the couch. Parker Jones was in his mid-twenties, with wild, unkempt hair, a green bomber jacket over an Irish sweater, and corduroys that led to his sneakers. Parker's sneakers and food were the only things he seemed to spend much money on.

The decor in their barren apartment was lacking. They had a single couch, coffee table, and TV mounted without any semblance of an entertainment unit underneath. The walls were bare, and the potential clients had to walk through this poor excuse of a living room in order to get to the actual office because, according to Parker, 'If we put the living room in that room, the only wall big enough for the TV would have a glare problem.' Of course, this didn't make sense for twenty-three and a half hours of the day because the apartment usually only got a half hour of light.

Beside Parker, there sat the other detective, Arlo. Arlo was a small black dog who looked more terrier than anything else, even though he was mostly sheep dog and Golden Retriever mix. Arlo was a distinctive canine, a black and white mutt with a too long body and a head too big for his short paws. He was mostly black, but his stomach, paws, mouth, and a small spot between his shoulder blades were all white. He rarely wore his collar in the apartment, preferring to leave it by the door. Unlike Parker, with his jacket and shoes, Arlo felt outdoor wear was best left at the door to separate the outside from the comfort of their home.

They were rewatching the local news for the third time that day, just hoping to glean something new from the crowd, from the street, or even from the reporter. The news reporter was a local legend around town. She covered all the best stories in the city because she'd earned it along with several Pulitzer Prizes and other accolades. Lin was in her 40s now and always wore the same beige trench coat, desert, or tundra. Lin seemed ageless somehow, with only a few whisps of white in her black hair. She was always ready to report which is why Parker always made sure to get on her good side. He and Arlo were always just behind the cameraman, waiting to investigate any breaking news.

It was the same story they'd been running all week. Someone had miraculously paved *another* entire street with chocolate. Children woke up to a Willy Wonka Wonderland, but pet owners woke up to a nightmare. The emergency vets were completely booked up, and they'd resorted to turning away patients who weren't violently ill.

The street behind her wasn't the first one that had been paved, and nobody thought it would be the last. This case had been ongoing for a month now. Each week, a new cul-de-sac was paved in chocolate overnight, with no witnesses and no clues. It was confounding Parker and Arlo. Neither could make sense of how there wasn't a single witness to a giant paver completely encasing a road in chocolate.

Lin began transitioning to the fluff of the story on TV as she shoved her mic in front of some locals who couldn't drive in to work because of the chocolate. "They're calling this mysterious character 'The Chocolatier.'" Lin began the interview, "Sir, you live here; what's your take on—" Parker turned off the TV before she could continue the interview. They'd gotten what they could out of rewatching the show—a whole lot of nothing.

Parker slapped his thighs, waking Arlo from his own musings as Parker announced, "Well. There's no use dwelling on it. We'll just have to go find some leads!" Parker was the optimist of the pair.

Arlo, on the other paw, knew better as he huffed back at Parker, "Sure, partner. Sure." But he stretched and hopped off the couch to follow Parker all the same. They didn't always see eye-to-eye, but Arlo didn't trust anyone in the entire world as much as Parker.

Parker sang them across their barren living room and opened the door to the office, "I bust a move; I bust a groove. I bust the perps; sometimes they're dogs. *Doo doo doo a chooka choo chooka choo.*"

The office space was fairly simple, though it was at least fully furnished and had some sort of decor on the walls. Even if that decor was photos and conspiracy boards with lines of yarn connecting cases: perps, criminals, and corrupt politicians alike. The room had two of everything in it, one large human-sized and one smaller dog-sized: two conspiracy boards, two desks, two lamps, and even two notepads. The only real difference in the room was that Arlo's desk had a bed, whereas Parker's had a chair. Arlo never did understand how humans could think like that, all hunched over.

Parker's conspiracy board was much sparser than Arlo's. He was working the case like every other private dick, hoping to crack it and land some more city gigs. So, his conspiracy board was all about 'The Chocolatier.' Unfortunately, they didn't have a lot to go on other than a silhouette with a question mark and four locations that were hit so far. The only real clue was that they were all cul-de-sacs. Nothing commercial had been hit by 'The Chocolatier.'

On Arlo's corkboard was a silhouette of a bone with a question mark, a few spots in a picture of a park, and a suspect list of about fifteen neighborhood dogs. It was a meaningless case from a Scottie down the road. Arlo suspected he'd get a bark that the Scottie had simply forgotten where he buried it. Still, the dog had paid his deposit, so they were retained. Arlo was nothing if not diligent.

Parker slumped down in his chair and swivelled to look at his own case as Arlo did circles to make his bed comfortable. "Arlo. I'll tell you, my man. I cannot make heads nor tails of this."

Arlo looked at his tail for a moment as he considered chasing it before responding, "Why do I feel like that's a dig at me?" He shook it off before laying his own head down. Staring at that corkboard wasn't going to solve anything. So, Arlo would just waited it out until Parker got antsy enough to actually go do some real investigating. Then, they could get something done. "I don't see what the big deal is, anyway. I love chocolate." Arlo knew in his heart that it was bad for him, but he couldn't help it. Chocolate was tasty.

Parker leaned back and let his head fall in exasperation. "I know. But, my guy, it will—I repeat, it *will* kill you."

Arlo just let his eyes close as he grunted back. "Worse ways to go out in this city. You know it was a negative twenty with the wind chill last night? I'd take chocolate over a night on the streets in that cold any day." Parker looked at the former stray. Arlo could see the sympathy. He knew it came from love, but it still irritated him. "It was six months. Don't look at me like that. Six months, I was on the street, and you came around. It was hot then, too. Stop looking at me like that."

Parker, never one to dwell on the negative, began to whistle as he flipped through his notebook and prepared his next song. "Dumb mutts dumb mutts. Whatcha gonna do? Whatcha gonna do when they eat their own poo?"

Arlo didn't even bother to lift his head as he responded to the teasing song, "You and the stereotypes," and let out his typical huff of exasperation.

Parker was completely unfazed as he began searching for something that Arlo couldn't care less about on the computer. Arlo knew Parker was able to use that machine for casework, but it did annoy the dog when Parker would spend hours on end on it. Parker just smiled and nodded his head as he readied yet another song, "Please. I am a stereo. Of glorious, beautiful." He switched to an awful screech of an attempt at a high note. "Musiiiiiiiiiic." Parker became more absorbed in what he was doing, so he whispered encouragement to himself, "Nailed it. And now. I'm gonna nail this case."

Arlo didn't even bother to lift his head as he muttered, so Parker couldn't hear, "You've tried the computer for hours. The answers aren't in our home. It's not like someone's gonna just come knocking on the door with the answers." Arlo perked up suddenly before he could continue down his pessimistic rabbit hole. He launched forward to the front door as someone was, in fact, knocking at the door.

Chapter 2
Someone Comes Knocking at the Door

Arlo completely lost his mind as he raced to the front door, barking. He never really knew why he did this, more often than not, he was happy to let the person knock in, but, on the off chance, it was a threat. Arlo wanted to be ready.

Parker was much softer on threat assessment than Arlo. He immediately launched after Arlo and attempted to calm him. "*Ey! Ey! Ey!* Cut it out! Shut up! No bark! Quiet!" Arlo didn't know why Parker refused to start with the word 'Quiet.' That was the command word they'd agreed to, for 'that's enough; the threat knows not to mess with us now.'

Arlo calmed himself down as he put his nose to the crack of the door, hoping to suss out who it was before Parker dragged him away from the door by his collar. It turned out to be the best-case scenario for Arlo. It wasn't a break in the case, but Arlo recognized the perfume of their upstairs neighbor from a mile away! Arlo liked Sally, so this was a good thing.

From Arlo's perspective, he'd been waiting nearly an eternity for this door to open. He was startled back to reality by Parker's leg suddenly jamming itself in front of his nose and blocking his access to the door. Sally called through the doorway in a panic, "Parker, you gotta help me out!"

Parker opened the door, and Sally strolled in without pause. Sally was around Parker's age, and it didn't matter the weather, she always dressed to impress. Today, she wore white dress gloves, a yellow summer dress, heels, and a pearl necklace. Unfortunately, for Arlo, she rarely came over without her dog in her arms. Toots was a Dachshund that Sally always dressed in a Tootsie Roll costume. Although the visual pun wasn't lost on Arlo, he thought it looked ridiculous, especially when paired with Toots' collar; the thing was ostentatious and looked more like a bib than a collar. With a giant diamond in the center, which Sally claimed was fake, but Arlo knew for a fact it was real and possibly worth more than the apartment building. He'd uncovered the truth about that the first week they moved in. Sally came from money, and it was a family heirloom. She supported herself and made her own way in the world, but her family had connections.

Sally put Toots down, and she immediately went over and peed on the curtains in the living room. Sally whipped around without even noticing the dog peeing and pleaded with Parker, "Toots' jabot is gone!"

Parker just crossed his arms as he watched Toots peeing in the corner and held Arlo's collar to keep him from going to pee on Toots' pee. He patiently waited for Sally to calm down a little before replying, "Her what?"

Sally threw her hands in the air in exasperation as Arlo tried to get out of Parker's grasp and run to her. She exclaimed aloud as she walked over to pet Arlo, "Her jabot! Her jabot!" The fact that she repeated the word didn't help Parker understand, so she took a deep breath and folded her arms. "Her collar."

Parker released Arlo as he put his hand to his face, finally understanding what Sally meant. "Oh. Well. Do they not make it anymore? You can probably—"

As Parker attempted to soothe Sally, Arlo jumped up and down, making sure not to get his paws on her dress, as he barked and whined, "It's you! It's you! It's you!"

Even as Sally dipped down to pet Arlo, she ignored his excitement to focus on the collar. "Honestly! You're a private detective. Surely, you knew I was lying about it being a fake diamond! I need it back! It was my great great great grandmother's aunt's gift from the King of France just before the French Revolution!"

Arlo couldn't help but laugh as he turned to Toots. "And you just kept it on your neck?" Toots, ever the snob, turned her nose to the air and ignored Arlo. So, Arlo went back to the joy of greeting Sally.

Parker walked into the kitchen before he came back into the living room with some stain remover and set to work cleaning the dog pee. He replied cautiously, "I dunno, Sal. I'm already kinda on a case."

Sally laughed as she put that idea down. "No! I just need you to watch Toots. Just while I find the collar! I'm not hiring you!"

Parker gave a singular laugh along with Sally, but Arlo suspected for a different reason. "Oh, that's even better."

As the humans figured out that mess, Arlo went over to the freshly cleaned corner and made sure to show Toots that this was his home. Covering her scent with his, he smirked at her as she ruffled her hair in protest. "This is actually mine!" He said as he walked over to her and finally gave her the customary dog greeting of smelling each another.

Parker set to work cleaning again. "Arlo! Come on!"

Even as he said this to Arlo, Sally was already halfway out the door. "Thanks so much! Buh bye!" With that, she closed the door behind her, leaving Toots with Arlo and Parker. Parker finished cleaning the corner for a second time.

Parker threw his head back and laughed again. "Great. Hey, Toots," he said as he pat her head.

Toots just threw her nose in the air and practically ignored Parker. Arlo looked at her quizzically. There'd never been any real kinship between him and her, but she was usually much more accepting of Parker. She liked Parker.

Toots pranced away from Parker and Arlo and hopped on their couch as she replied, "The collar's not really even worth it in my opinion."

Parker grabbed his hat by the entryway, tightened his shoelaces as he readied to leave, and called out to the newcomer, "Convince Sally of that?" Toots just scoffed, and Parker shook his head, laughing once more. He took things in stride, and Arlo respected that. However, Arlo didn't like to see Toots scoffing at them like they were lesser.

Arlo walked up and put his nose to Toots, growling warningly, "You know we live in the same place; they spend the same money on rent, and we work just as hard in this city as you and Sally."

Toots sneered as she turned her nose once more. "No. You've been here since before the gentrification. We got in while it was hot. More money." Arlo repulsed with what she'd just said so confidently and with such pride.

He hopped next to her on the couch and nudged her off, so she was standing now. Slowly, he herded her to the door as he confusedly asked, "Are you bragging about spending more on rent for the same building?"

"I'm bragging that we have more money to spend," Toots replied haughtily.

Parker rolled his eyes in good humor as he put one foot out the door and turned to Arlo. "Hey, buddy. It'd really help a lot if you could take care of this."

"And the dame?" Arlo cocked his head to indicate he was talking about Toots.

Parker laughed once more and ruffled Arlo's head as he made one last remark before exiting, "That's my guy. I've gotta go check out this latest scene while it's still hot. Hopefully, we missed something, and we can get the ball rolling on this case. Look for her collar or something. You don't have a case right now anyway, besides that Scotty's lost bone." Parker left the door open for Arlo in case the dog wanted to leave too.

Arlo and Toots eyed each other warily as Arlo grabbed his collar, threw it in the air, and let it fall around his neck. "Well, Toots? Let's go find your collar. How hard can it be to find something you probably just dropped?"

Chapter 3
Much Harder Than He Thought

Toots strolled out of the apartment as Arlo rolled his eyes and followed. As they exited the building, Arlo finally asked, "So, where'd you lose the collar?"

Toots continued on without so much as a glance at him as she barked back, "We'll go to the park if we must look for it, and I didn't lose anything. It must have been a grand heist planned for weeks to get the jewel." The two dogs made their way to the park, and Arlo continuously stopped to smell every flower and pee on every post along the way. It made for a long walk.

Finally, they arrived at their destination; the park was the largest park in the city. The sun shone through dark gray clouds, making it look more like the moon. The trees were a deep green, and the benches lined the main path as the two dogs made their way past pedestrians heading home for the night. The exodus from the park was like rush hour, and the two dogs and several rats were on a reverse commute as Arlo asked Toots, "Where do you last remember having it?"

Toots made her way to a clearing and put her nose to the ground as she mumbled back, "I don't know. I guess when we played fetch?" To Arlo, it didn't seem like she was particularly interested in recovering the missing collar. She was hiding something. He could feel it deep in his paws. This case was thick with dirt, and Arlo—he was just chasing the garbage truck. "Let's just go to Juise and get some pawsitively banana smoothies!" Toots excitedly threw the idea out there.

Arlo rolled his eyes at her pun as she jolted him from his musing. "What are you, an ad for them? I don't go for that stuff. What about that local joint, Ruff's?"

Toots just sauntered away and awkwardly pooped. She didn't even seem to entertain the idea, as she let nature take its course. She threw contradictory statements at Arlo as she pooped, "Look away. Look away. But look near me. But not at me. Look away, but near me! Okay? Eye contact! Eye contact! No eye contact! Look away! But at me! Near me! Near me—at me—near. At. There! There!" Arlo was used to this, and it was one of the reasons he preferred people to dogs. Some instinct of needing to feel safe demanded this awkward ritual of shame and pack mentality while pooping. He did his best to follow along with her instructions as she stared at him while pooping. He may not have liked it, but he was still a decent dog who didn't want anyone to feel unsafe. The city was unsafe enough without him turning his back on everyone. Toots finished up and began kicking dirt behind her. "*Ugh.* Ruff's is grosser than what I just buried," she continued their conversation as though it weren't just interrupted.

Arlo became indignant. It was a locally owned great place! "Ruff's isn't gross! It's got soul. You can feel the community there, not like Juise. Corporations like that are the reason so many places around here are losing their—"

Toots completely shut him down as she'd heard him go on about corporations in the past, "Yeah, yeah, yeah. I've heard it all. Whatever. You know Sally's father is rich and sits on the board of Juise. He's a big deal, and if you ever try it, maybe you'd realize what quality tastes like and why it became a chain. Because everybody loves it." There it was again, her nose in the air as she soaked in her own superiority.

Arlo just muttered under his breath with a growl, "You and Juise have the gross-on-the-inside thing in common." He put his nose to the ground and tracked what scent remained of Toots and Sally playing earlier in the day. "Now show me where you were when it disappeared."

Toots ran off, forcing Arlo to sprint after her. Despite himself, he couldn't help but enjoy this little bit as they ran through the open park. He wasn't sure how he felt about enjoying it, so he began zig-zagging behind and in front of her and barking at her. Letting his sheepdog out, he stopped her from running, and they both calmed down as they panted with tongues out.

"She threw it from here!" Toots took off again as she excitedly continued their odd little game of fun and fun-ruining. Once again, Arlo's hesitation to enjoy his time put an end to the zoomies, and Toots panted out. "What? Was your great-grandma an Aussie or somethin'? Come on!"

Arlo just nodded and reminded here, "We're here to work, not to play." Then he pointed to the ground. "This about where you lost it?"

Toots put her own nose to the ground and smelled alongside him. "A sheepdog detective. What happened to the good ol' days when you private dicks were all hounds? A nose like that, and we'd have the answer by now."

Arlo ignored the jab and continued hounding her with questions, "Did you see anyone?"

Toots scoffed at this. Arlo knew why, of course, she saw someone. They were at a public park. Still, he waited until she replied, "Sure, I did! But no one's butt smelled suspicious."

Arlo tried to keep her talking. She was definitely being cagey about this whole thing. "Any shifty figures, I mean." Toots shook her head no. Arlo stopped and smelled one tree in particular. Toots raced over to him and sat right at the foot of the tree, very stiff and upright. He tried sniffing around her, but she wouldn't move, so he had to go around her. "You were here for sure. I smell you." He went on.

Toots nodded but kept her stiff posture. "Oh, great, now you *do* think you're a hound. Following that nose, think you'll track my whole day?"

Arlo looked around for anything out of the ordinary— anything that could lead them in the right direction. He honed in on a tree with a pretty solid vantage point from most of the angles in the area, with a small flock loitering about. He also spotted a 'Juise' store visible across the street and working inside was Purrcella, an old friend who sometimes acted a bit… catty. Finally, he spotted a traffic light with a camera on it.

Arlo decided the first stop would be the birds. "Follow me," he said to Toots as he strutted over to the birds. He'd have to do his best not to bark at them. Toots waited a moment before she finally left her little seated stoop. They approached the tree, and Arlo couldn't help but hop his front two paws up the tree like a dog chasing a squirrel. He wanted to get the birds and bring them back to Parker with every bone in his body. "Hey! Hey, you guys! Birds!" he called up the tree to the birds. They ignored him completely as Arlo began to think he'd hit a wall. No bird was gonna sing in this case.

Toots seemed to try to steer them away once again as she whined to Arlo, "How do we even know they were here or saw—" However, she was interrupted as three of the birds hopped down from the tree once they spotted Toots.

Three crows with hats and gloves on flew down from their perch. One wore red, one wore blue, and one wore green. Arlo began to wonder if it was a bad parody of Ducktales. The one with the red hat on stuck its wing out to the one in green as it cawed, "Hey Jerry, ain't that the cat from this morning?"

The crow dressed in green, Jerry, replied almost instantly, "Nah, Larry. That's a dog."

The crow dressed in blue took three short hops forward as it joined the conversation. "I think she looks more like a piece of candy, fellas." The blue crow brushed its wing on Toots' Tootsie Roll costume as though the others wouldn't know what he was talking about. These were a few bold crows to hop right up to two dogs like this, Arlo thought.

Larry replied again, "*Eh,* shuddup, Terry." So, the green one was Jerry, the red one was Larry, and the blue one was Terry. Arlo felt that this was all unnecessarily confusing.

Jerry came to Terry's defense as he hopped back into the mix, "Don't be mean to Terry, Larry." Finally, one of the three stooge crows introduced themselves to the dogs, "Hi. Name's Jerry." Jerry stuck out a wing like a handshake, and Arlo stepped forward, sniffing. It was only customary for dogs to sniff any newcomer after all, but this seemed to worry the birds as they all hopped back in unison.

Arlo grinned, a toothy grin showing off his canines. "A little jumpy? Got somethin' to hide?" he asked the flighty birds.

Toots took this opportunity to step in and apologized for Arlo, much to his chagrin, "Sorry about him; he used to be a street mutt. Gets wary when he meets new fellas. Name's Toots; he's Arlo. We're with Arlonius Investigations." This was news to Arlo that she suddenly counted herself as part of Arlonius Investigations, but if it moved the case along, he'd allow it for now without correction.

Terry peaked around Toots' shoulder at Arlo, so Arlo just laid down and licked his paws. Toots wanted to take over the interrogation. All the better for Arlo, he wasn't a big fan of trying to talk to strangers.

Larry took the lead for the birds once more as he squawked, "Sure, Toots. Pleasure's mine. These two are Jerry and Terry." As they were more formally introduced, they stepped forward and each gave a little bow before Larry continued on, "You lookin' for that bipedal? The one you threw the ball around with? We just saw her pass by this way not too long ago. We can…"

Arlo knew these birds were the culprits. He jumped right in and interrupted Larry before the bird could go on. "Observant, ain't ya? Maybe seen somethin' you thought you'd like to have—"

Toots immediately interrupted the excited dog and smoothed things over quickly enough that the birds barely had time to unruffle their feathers. "No, no, nothing like that. We're both just here looking for my collar. We wanted to see if you'd seen anything."

Terry piped up this time extraordinarily proudly, "I seens lotsa stuff!"

Jerry continued the thought as though it were his own, but much more somber, "But ain't nothin useful."

Larry seemed to be the pragmatist of the bunch as he took the lead again. "Well, hold on, Jerry. Nice dog like this; let's see if we can help. Terry, what'd ya see?"

Terry immediately listed everything he'd seen that day, "I seen seventeen bikers, three old ladies (they're my favorite with the bread ooooooooooweeee), a couple of families, two picnics (one went swell, the other not so much), a dog playin' fetch in a costume (hey, that was you!) I seen a cat with three eyes, which I thought was weird, but ya know I'm not one to judge. And I seen three other bikers come by after the first seventeen (they were the morning bikers.) I saw someone buy a bag a' oregano."

Terry didn't pause for a breath as Larry gently pushed him aside. Terry just kept rattling off things he'd seen as Larry apologized, "Sorry, Toots. Sorry, Arbo. Nothin' we seen gonna be helpful for ya."

Arlo haughtily stood and stalked off as he called back insincerely, "Well, thanks for nothing." He considered letting that end it, but he still felt indignant at the unnecessary jab from the bird, so he corrected Larry too, "And it's Arlo!" The birds cackled at this as though it were the height of comedy. Toots thanked them again before she followed Arlo back across the park to the street.

When she caught up with Arlo, she said almost proudly, "Well. That was a waste," the dogs continued as they heard Terry still listing things he'd seen grow quieter and quieter with distance.

Arlo grinned at Toots as he revealed the truth of the matter, "Starting to feel like you don't want us to find that collar. Those birds gave me everything I needed." The cat with three eyes, Arlo, knew exactly who that was. He held a bush aside with a paw to reveal the Juise bar across the street to Toots before continuing. "I got a friend who works there. Looks to me like she's outta the pound, and it sounds to me like she made a little trip into the park today." Across the street and serving a smoothie to a person was Purrcella. Purrcella was a mostly white cat with black paws and a diamond patch of black on her forehead. Like a reverse Arlo, he was certain that this cat burglar had something to do with this case.

Chapter 4
With Friends Like These, Who Needs Enemies?

The dachshund and the mutt looked both ways before they crossed the street. Arlo knew what he was getting into with this cat, but Toots needed to be prepared, so he gave her the lowdown. "Purrcella's slick and quick, fast and feline; she's a thief, but she rarely gets caught. She's not a villain, but she's not a good guy either. Right now, she's suspect numero uno." Toots nodded along as they reached Juise. Arlo could tell she wasn't paying attention.

The sidewalk outside was the usual city gray, but the store itself was full of oranges, pinks, and yellows. The smoothie shop looked almost like a tech company hangout, with the trademark graffiti title 'Juise' spray painted on the sign and visible through the massive walls of glass on the far wall. Arlo noted that each staff member smiled and greeted them the moment they came in, but he also saw how those smiles dissipated the moment the staff turned away. They were well-trained goons paid just enough by some committee of millionaires to put up with the abuse customer service representatives were forced to endure. Oh, sure, Juise toted itself as different. It even had a dedication to rehabilitation, which explained why

Purrcella had a job there as an ex-convict. Still, Arlo didn't trust any place where the owners themselves weren't front and center, at least one day out of the week. The two dogs walked right up to the cat at the register, and Arlo greeted her like an old friend, "Hey there, sister. How ya doin'?"

Purrcella, unlike the other employees, didn't smile as she replied, "Whatdya want Arlo? Can't you see I'm a workin' stiff since I got out? I don't know nothin' 'bout whatever you're sniffin'." With that, Purrcella took a rag and wiped down the counter busily.

Arlo wasn't put off by this greeting at all. She may not have reacted to Toots being there, which might indicate innocence, but she still had the opportunity, the motive, and the means to commit the crime. He leaned on the counter as the rag swept by and pretended to pick at his teeth when he spoke again, "Come on, slick. Who ya tryin' to fool? Just got a few questions is all." He idly tried to act like she *wasn't* his main suspect.

Purrcella looked at Toots with distrust and asked, "Who's this little sweetheart?" Arlo squinted at her as he wondered if, maybe, the basic math wasn't adding up after all.

Toots surprised Arlo when she pushed him out of the way and leaned right into Purrcella's face, "Name's Toots. Who's the mangy feline?" Her question was directed at Arlo, like she wasn't staring Purrcella's down.

Arlo pulled her aside with concern. He didn't want to start a fight, just a conversation. So, he whispered to Toots, "You were so good with the crows. Bring a little of that here."

Toots didn't look away from Purrcella as she muttered out of the side of her mouth, "I'm good with everyone. I read animals." Arlo found that hard to believe. How could coming in with such a challenging attitude possibly result in anything but getting shut down?

Much to Arlo's surprise, Purrcella laughed and flipped the rag back onto her shoulder. "All right. Toots it is." With that, Purrcella came around the side and walked to the employee's only section. As she went, she called back, "Meet me in the alley." Then, she yelled to another employee working a blender, "I'm taking a ten. Watch the front for me, will ya?"

Arlo took a moment to look at Toots. This was twice now that she'd figured out how to get someone to talk. Arlo began to wonder if he'd misjudged her as a spoiled princess with old money. He even wondered if he should take her around the next chocolate street scene to see if she could get anyone talking that he and Parker couldn't. He thought this as they made their way toward the back alley, but when they got around back, he stopped thinking and was jolted back to reality.

Behind, Juise wasn't as refined. The waiters on break arm wrestled and gambled in the alleyway with dice and cards. Every eye fell on Arlo and Toots as Toots muttered to Arlo, "I don't think we're welcome here."

Arlo may have suspected Purrcella, but he knew roughing folks up wasn't her modus operandi, so he tried to soothe Toots' concerns. "Purrcella's tricky, but she won't get us hurt…" He paused as he remembered the last time he'd talked with Purrcella and ended up dangling from a bridge for an hour. "Too bad." He finished unconvincingly.

Purrcella came through the back door and scratched and rubbed against the wall. She was one cool cat and acted like this was her place. "So?"

Arlo understood, straight to business. So, he answered just as simply, "It's a collar."

Purrcella stopped and looked at Arlo as she came up to him and compared their sizes before she smirked, "I didn't know you turned bounty hunter."

Arlo realized she thought he meant bringing in a perp of interest, so he clarified, "A jeweled collar. Just the kinda thing you'd love to get your sticky paws all over." There it was, he'd laid it down for her to pick up; she was his suspect.

She didn't react much to the antagonistic bait. Purrcella just looked at her nails and filed them down on the wall as her words oozed out, "*Hmm.* So, a collar goes missing, and I'm suspect number one? Well, my paws got fresh juice on 'em and that's it. No jewelry, I ain't risking goin' back in the clink." She winked at the dogs. "At least, not so soon."

Arlo didn't back down, though. She seemed innocent. Still, maybe if he pressed a bit more, "Collar's worth a lot of money. Seems to me—"

Before he could go on, Toots interrupted him, "*Uh,* Arlo. I think it's time for us to—" She diverted his attention enough to notice they'd been surrounded by the other employees.

Arlo wasn't ready to call it, though. "We're fine." He turned his attention back to Purrcella as though they weren't being intimidated. "You're bold; I'll give ya that. But it's all there, Purrc: opportunity, motive, and means. Witness saw you in the park, opportunity. Collar's worth a fortune, and you'd spot that a mile away, motive. You're the best thief in the city, and you saw some dumb, rich dog playing a game. It'd be so easy for you to snake one of those claws around that collar and swipe from the shadows, means." He was right. Those were all possibilities. However, when he said it aloud, he couldn't shake that it didn't *feel* right.

Purrcella was just as apathetic about the interrogation as she was before. Completely unfazed, she shooed Arlo and Toots as though they were flies. Then, dramatically, she fell back and raised her paw to her forehead like some terrible victim of accusation. "I ain't your cat. Your witness must've seen me from the park over here. I haven't stepped paw over that street. My life of crime's behind; it's in the past." She headed to the door, but Arlo put his paw on her tail and stopped her in her tracks. The crowd didn't seem to like it either, as he saw that a few bore their fangs and growled at him for his action. He had to press on, though. "Come on, Purrc, not so fast."

A Chow in particular, with some smoothie bits stuck in its fur, stepped forward and loomed over Arlo. "We played some cards. Everyone seen. She didn't take no necklace under no tree."

Arlo waited until the Chow had its face in his before replying, "You're a crook, a snake; most of you are villainous. You've all been locked up, spit out, and can't wait to go back to the pound." Arlo didn't believe what he was saying as fact. He hoped he was wrong. He wasn't always an upstanding citizen himself, but he wanted to provoke them. Throw them off and get at the truth.

Purrcella moved to the Chow's defense and pointed her claw at Arlo's chest, poking and pushing until his back was against the wall. She accused, "You're chasing shadows, without real work. I'm just a store clerk. You've been there, too. You know what it's like. I know all about your past, Arlo, and I won't let you act like you're better than any o' the rest of us." Toots looked at Arlo with some confusion, but Arlo ignored it.

Toots knew he was from the streets, but she didn't know much about the first year of his life. She didn't know about his stint with the police, his undercover work, or how it all went wrong. She didn't need to know, so he ignored her look and nodded to Purrcella. The cat burglar was right. "You're the easy answer. I want that to be right. Occam's Razer and all that. But I believe you." Purrcella didn't say anything as she left them in the alley with unfriendly faces. Arlo didn't blame her; he'd accused her without doing the due diligence a private investigator should. He'd hoped to catch an easy confession, but his investigation had been clumsily handled so far. Somberly, he led Toots away from the crowd, which went back to cackling and gambling.

The dogs rounded a corner, and Arlo looked at his last lead: the camera on the street might have caught something. He'd need Parker's help for that. He didn't have access to that kind of thing, but there were websites and forms Parker could fill out to get them from the city. Arlo felt defeated, until he noticed a not-so-subtle surveillance van. Maybe he didn't need Parker's help after all. He walked with purpose once more. Toots almost pleaded behind him, "Maybe it's time to throw in the towel? Sally'll get over it." But Arlo wasn't ready to throw in the towel just yet.

Chapter 5
Canines and K9s

The two dogs walked up to the van, and Arlo asked Toots a question, "Did you know your picture's taken seventy-five times a day on average?"

Toots didn't seem impressed by his fun fact, "Including selfies?"

Arlo pressed on as though she had been enthusiastic, "Who do you think has access to that stuff? Find the right dog, find the right camera, and you've got access to the whole story." As he spoke, Arlo pointed to the traffic camera that he hoped had some of the park in its view. Toots looked at the camera, and her tail fell to the ground in disappointment. Arlo didn't know why she wanted so badly to kill this investigation. It was her jewel he was trying to find. He supposed it was just like how Sally hadn't hired Parker. These snobs didn't think of Arlo and Parker as professionals.

Toots protested, "Well, how do we even get access to something like—"

Arlo interrupted her by knocking on the unmarked white van they stood outside of. The door immediately swung open, and both dogs were dragged inside. The door closed, and Arlo waited for his eyes to adjust to the darkness inside the van.

The only light emitted in the van was from two computer monitors. One showed footage of an entryway to Rip's Garage down the street. More of a junkyard, Rip was a known thug who ran most of the crime throughout the city. This was a police surveillance unit. The other monitor showed the back entry to the same facility. This was a sting operation that Arlo and Toots had stumbled into. The canine in charge of this surveillance was a German Shepherd K9 unit that Arlo knew well. McMack always looked like he was so stiff and domineering in his K9 vest, but Arlo knew the big dog was a big softy.

McMack whined immediately to Arlo, "Why do you wanna get me fired?"

Arlo couldn't help but wag his tail a little. He had little love for the police, but McMack was the closest thing Arlo had to a friend in the dog world. "Hey, Mack!"

Toots must've been too stunned to speak or realize what was going on because she started barking and slammed into the walls of the van, "HELP DOGNAPPING! I'M TOO LAP DOG TO BE OUT ON THE STREET! I WON'T SURVIVE!"

McMack and Arlo just watched her for a while with raised eyebrows. When Toots finally calmed down enough to see that Arlo wasn't concerned, the old friends began sniffing eachothers' butts. McMack asked Arlo, "How'd you even—"

Arlo knew what he was going to ask before he finished, so he cut in, "Your tailing's always been a little

off, Mack. I spotted you from across the street. Subtlety's
not your strong suit."

McMack's tail stopped wagging as Toots finally
joined the conversation, "What's going on?"

Arlo introduced the two dogs, "Officer McMack.
Toots. He's running a surveillance op on Rip's Garage it
looks like?" Arlo asked as he leered over McMack's
shoulder to get a better look.

McMack blocked as much of Arlo's view as he could,
and he gritted his teeth. "We'll catch that Pitbull. Just you
wait."

Toots, at least, wasn't completely oblivious to the
city's going ons. "Hey, I saw that on the news! Didn't he
just do a stint?" She was surprising Arlo left and right with
how capable she'd been today. He decided he'd misjudged
her as just some spoiled brat. She was a spoiled brat, but
she was more than that too.

McMack seemed crestfallen about Rip's stint in the
pound. "For tax evasion. We gotta get him on something
bigger, though. He bites a lotta dogs and a lotta people, but
we can never pin him." He shook his paw in the air.

Arlo put a paw on McMack's shoulder as he calmed
the large dog. "You will, pal. I believe in you." But the
moment McMack looked away, Arlo shook his head to
Toots. Arlo liked McMack a lot, but Rip wasn't going to
be taken down by a sweet and loyal dog. Rip would be
taken down by something or someone much darker in
nature. "Anywho. I was hoping you'd be able to help me
with some traffic footage." Arlo recaptured McMack's
attention with that.

McMack looked down at the ground like he'd been asked to do something awful. "Come on, Arlo. Chief hates you. Don't ask me to stick my neck out like this. Not again." This German Shepherd did know how to whine.

Arlo, though, knew just how to get his pal to fold. "Please, Mack? For old time's sake."

McMack sheepishly swiped his tail back and forth as he considered, "I don't remember them being all that great."

Arlo pushed Toots in front of McMack. "Then for Toots here? A sweet dachshund like her? Can't an officer help a citizen these days?" If their friendship wasn't going to get him what he wanted, maybe McMack's desire to help the citizens of their city would. "Or is the city so—"

McMack interrupted with the realization, "And another thing! You brought a civy into my operation here? I'm trying to be stealthy!" He shifted his head back and forth to indicate stealth.

Arlo couldn't help but take the low hanging fruit as he wryly replied, "And failing."

Arlo immediately felt bad as McMack's head fell, but the dog bounced back quickly. "*Ugh.* Fine. What's wrong?"

P.I. Arlo took the reins again as friend-lo stepped aside. Back to business. "She's got a collar's gone missing." Arlo answered dutifully.

Now it was McMack's turn to be sardonic, "Well, stop the press. A collar! Golly gee."

Toots became indignant pretty quickly as she jumped in McMack's face. "It has a diamond! A really valuable one! Worth more than all the tech in this turd of a van, for sure!"

McMack was a trained professional; he didn't rise just because those around him had flared tempers, "Well, why'd ya go and lose something like that?"

Toots pouted. "I didn't lose it!"

Arlo decided to step back. "It was stolen. Funny how the Chief's fancy words aren't actually stopping any crime."

McMack sat up on two legs and waved his two front paws like a show dog in an attempt to calm Arlo and Toots. "All right. All right." The German Shepherd went to the computer screen and typed on it using the three paw-shaped buttons designed for K9 units. After a series of clicks, the traffic footage popped up on one of the monitors. Sure enough, the park could be seen just at the edge of where Arlo suspected the collar was stolen. "What time are we lookin for?"

Arlo looked at Toots. She shrugged and replied vaguely, "This morning?"

McMack sighed. "Any more exact time?"

Arlo replied for her this time, "Her morning walk's 8.30 a.m. to 8.35 a.m. out the door. Would've taken fifteen minutes or so to get here."

Toots looked as though Arlo had struck her. "Stalker!"

Arlo just sighed in a defeated manner, like he'd explained this a thousand times before. "Detective. I notice patterns."

Toots scoffed, "Some detective you are. Can't even find—"

McMack interrupted, "Here we are!" He pointed at the monitor. He'd scrubbed the portion of the day where Toots periodically came into frame as she retrieved a frisbee and brought it back off screen. It was hard to make out, but Arlo could see the collar was still there. She went around behind the tree they'd investigated earlier, and, sure enough, when she came back out a few moments later, the collar was gone.

Arlo became completely dejected as he watched Toots return and fetch over and over without the collar. "Thanks, Mack." Arlo moped.

McMack immediately took on Arlo's mood as though it were his own. "Why so glum? We got the exact time it disappeared." He tried to shine some optimism on the situation.

Arlo just pointed to the tree. "That tree. We checked it out already. I peed on it too. Dead end. Thanks anyway, pal." Arlo opened the surveillance door and gestured for Toots to leave.

Just before the door closed behind them, McMack called out, "You're the best graduate from the academy. You'll get 'em."

Chapter 6
Arlo Doesn't Get Them

Arlo and Toots walked silently down the street. When they got to the end of the commercial district, they found themselves outside of the very garage that McMack was surveilling. Outside a chain link fence across the street, Arlo sat down, and Toots followed suit. Arlo's mind reeled; he didn't want to visit Rip. They'd hit a crossroads, and he didn't have any leads. If the diamond was as valuable as he suspected, Rip was sure to have heard of it being moved in the city. Nothing valuable got moved without him knowing something. "Listen, Toots." Arlo began, "This whole thing's been more fun than I thought it would be. I thought it'd be a chore." He could tell immediately that she was offended, but he didn't know why. He'd just paid her a compliment, after all.

Toots sarcastically responded, "Thanks for sharing that. Glad I'm not a total letdown to you."

Arlo sighed and looked to the sky. "That's not my point." He paused as he tried to figure out what he was trying to say. "It's been fun, but it's also been safe. It's not safe in there." Arlo pointed across the street to Rip's Garage.

Toots looked at Rip's Garage, and decidedly nodded. "I mean, the cops are here too, right?"

Arlo could tell she didn't know about this world. He tried his best to explain, "As far as that dog's concerned"—he pointed into the garage—"They don't have jurisdiction in there. They'd have to see you in trouble on camera to do anything, and even then… It'd be a discussion for them. They care more about their ops than dogs like us."

Arlo could tell Toots didn't believe him as she said, "McMack seemed to care."

McMack did care, and Arlo knew that. However, Arlo also knew that McMack had very little authority on the matter with a big fish like Rip on the line. Arlo patiently walked through his words, "Yeah. He cares, but he doesn't make the decisions." Toots didn't seem to care as she started walking across the street. "I'm serious, Toots." Arlo stopped her with one paw off the sidewalk. "I can't guarantee your safety in there. Next time, if there is one. This is just the last lead I can think of. It's my last resort here. This dog makes Purrcella's crowd seem like house cats." Arlo's words weren't the most thought out, as he struggled to explain why he couldn't put a civilian like her at risk. Especially when he knew Rip was likely to be worse than usual at the sight of Arlo.

Toots continued her protest, but Arlo could tell he'd gotten to her with his loss for words. "But…"

Arlo put a paw on her shoulder and gave her the credit she was due all day. "You did great today. I'm gonna go in and follow up this last lead. Head home to Sally, and buck up. I'll get your collar back." With that, Arlo crossed the street, and a few rats scurried out of his way and into the gutters.

He didn't get far as Toots tenaciously grabbed his tail in her mouth. "Wait! He won't know anything." She protested with a mouth full of tail.

Arlo chuckled in response. "Don't talk with your mouth full. If anyone knows anything, it'll be him. A jewel like that? He'll have a paw in it down the line somewhere. Plus, he owes me one. I took the case. That means I see it through to the end, no matter what. That's what being a private detective means." He pulled his tail free and moved across the street.

Toots muttered after him, just audibly, "But it's my fault."

This wasn't the same spoiled brat Arlo thought he'd known. And yet, it was. He just hadn't looked past that before. He muttered to himself, "Poor kid, blaming herself." He went on to steel himself for the position he'd soon be in. His thoughts reeled, *Maybe I'm just a small dog in a humans' world, but everybody's got their pride, right? Even a spoiled brat like that didn't want to turn away from the most notorious thug in the city.* Arlo reached the other side of the street, just outside of the chain link fence, he looked in the direction he knew the camera to be. He waved and gave a cheeky grin. Arlo made his way onto the property of Rip's Garage.

Two of Rip's Chihuahua goons stood guard just like always, Charlie and Franky. Rip liked to surround himself with aggressive dogs, and few dogs were as in your face as Chihuahuas. The two dogs grinned maliciously at Arlo as he approached the doorway past the chain link fence, and Charlie said, "Ain't seen yous 'round in a while."

Franky puffed himself up and tried to meet Arlo's eye line. "Boss won't wanna see ya."

Charlie walked circles around Arlo as he measured him up with his eyes. "You're smaller than you used to be. Less in shape too. Smart plays stayin' outta his hair long as he ain't followin' up wit' yous."

Arlo took a deep breath and considered taking the high road, but then he looked at the Chihuahua circling him and decided to aggravate it instead. "He still only employing the most aggressive type of dogs I see. Doesn't matter how small they are I guess. Just dumb and mean."

Franky didn't like that as he puffed himself up even more. "What'd you say?!"

Charlie stopped circling Arlo and went to calm his partner. "He's just blowin' steam, Franky. Let him. Ya know what? Boss' schedule just opened up for you." Charlie was trying to punish Arlo, but it didn't matter because Arlo had a case to solve.

Arlo grinned back toward the camera for one last look before he headed through the doors.

He entertained the idea of what McMack's face must look like, and it made Arlo chuckle to himself.

There were massive piles of scrap inside the building. Cars, bicycles, anything and everything with gears were littered around the place in semi-organized piles. There was a beefy Pitbull with denim overalls and gold chains that sat atop a Cadillac at the back end of the yard. Rip had piercings on his short ears and didn't look all that thrilled to see Arlo walk in.

Arlo approached the center of the indoor junkyard and stepped into a sort of spotlight. Back when he worked with Rip, he was the one who'd set up this spotlight. A way to not-so-subtly put whoever came to talk to Rip at a disadvantage. It was just a bigger version of the classic police interrogation method of putting a lamp in someone's face. Rip waited patiently for Arlo to say something as the thug gnawed a large elk bone.

Arlo wasn't sure how to start and knew he'd have to talk first. Rip used every power play in the book to gain the upper hand in all interactions. "Hey, Rip, long time no see." Arlo kept his nerves steel and looked Rip right in the eyes.

Rip paused and measured Arlo up and down before his gravelly voice gruffed, "You got some nerve showing your mug around here."

Arlo shrugged back like it was no big deal. "I'm following a case. You're the last guy who'll know somethin' about it." He paused and tilted his head before he added impudently, "I gotta ask, right?"

Rip never liked Arlo's attitude much when it was pointed his way. He closed his eyes and slowly opened them in irritation. His voice was strained this time with an effort to remain calm. "Yeah? And why shouldn't I give you a trip to Aunt Patty's farm right now in the back of this trunk?" Rip patted the car as he stood up. He wasn't the largest dog in the world, but his presence was always intimidating.

Arlo hooked a paw and gestured back as he offered something he figured Rip already knew. "The fuzz is monitoring the entrances. Did you know that?"

Rip didn't take this well as he growled. "That a threat? Thought you didn't run with them anymore. Cut ties with them the same time you did with me, or was that all a lie too? Hard to tell the truth with a dog you don't trust."

Arlo sat down and held his head high. He knew what he'd walked into, and he needed to subvert the anger Rip had for him. "Just trading info."

Rip gestured to the door and offered Arlo an out. "Then bring me something I don't already know. That all you got? Or is it time to say goodbye?" Arlo was surprised; he was even offered the door.

Still, he needed to get any information he could. He ignored the out, and pressed on. "How about helping an old friend?"

As quickly as he was offered the door, that window was closed. Rip shot daggers with his eyes as venom spit from his mouth, "Point 'em out, and I'll be sure to help them."

Arlo casually paced the spotlight as he took in his surroundings. "Fine, we have history, and I didn't wanna do this, but" he spotted places in the room he could jump to where Rip wouldn't be able to get him. He needed to buy time if the next sentence spoiled everything. It was time for Arlo to gamble—"You owe me." He braced his legs, ready to leap if Rip launched.

However, Rip hopped down and stalked menacingly toward Arlo instead. Arlo couldn't show fear, so he stood stock still until Rip was breathing down his nape.

Rip repeated Arlo's words back to him as a challenge, "I owe *you*?"

Arlo knew this was an uphill battle. He gritted his teeth and said as strongly as he could, "I spent six months on the street, and you weren't put away. I made sure of that."

Rip looped a claw under Arlo's collar and pulled Arlo off his two front paws to eye level. "Way I figure it," Rip said, "you betrayed me. You landed a cushy home. You work the private sector now. And you still owe me a job. And I let you walk away without a fuss, something I don't do. Do I have that all right?"

"I don't do that anymore," Arlo said, strained, as the collar choked his neck.

Rip let Arlo down, and he smoothed out Arlo's fur around his shoulders. Rip then walked behind and smelled Arlo's butt. With this, Arlo visibly relaxed. This was like breaking bread for humans. "So, I've heard," Rip began. "But you came at a good time. I got a job for a private eye. Nothin' too dirty. Just help me out. I'm bein' set up and could use a real snake in the grass that knows how to uncover anything at any cost." Arlo read the subtext. Rip thought he was being set up by someone in the police and wanted Arlo to play both sides like last time.

Arlo couldn't outright refuse. This might be his only chance, but he had to see if there was anything else. "I have a case. That's why I'm here. Try the cops if you need some

investigating. I'm sure they'll jump at the chance to—"
Rip walked to the car and hopped back onto the trunk
before he laid down and stopped Arlo with a glare. Arlo
gulped and continued, "You help me with this case, and I
can wrap it up. Then, I'll hear out your case. I'm not taking
it if it smells anything like the past, though."

Rip laughed and flipped the elk bone into the air
repeatedly while they talked.

In the air, the bone went. "Sure, Arlo. Deal." And he
caught the bone.

So, they had a deal, and Arlo would finally figure out
where the diamond was. "You heard anything about a
diamond being hocked?"

In the air, the bone went. "Plenty." And he caught the
bone.

Arlo was sick of this game, but he wouldn't get
anything extra. He had to ask the exact questions that
would get him the exact answers. "I'm talking about a real
valuable one. I'm talking life changing to priceless in
value. Anything like that?" Arlo asked.

In the air, the bone went. "A diamond like that would
be trouble." And he caught the bone.

"You don't want trouble," Arlo offered as an
incentive to go on.

In the air, the bone went. "Looks like you made the
deal for nothin'. Haven't heard of anything like that
moving in the city, and I'd be the first to hear." This time
he let the bone land and held it up between his paws.

Arlo felt it prudent not to mention that he was certain
a thief like Purrcella would actually hear about it first. So,

instead, he offered his gratitude to the mob boss, "Yeah. Well. Thanks anyway, I guess."

Rip laughed maliciously at some unknown joke. "Made a deal with the devil for nothin'." He laughed mirthfully at Arlo's misfortune.

Arlo just shook his head and muttered, "Something like that." Rip didn't used to laugh at misfortune. Had their past really changed him so much?

Arlo turned to leave, but Rip called him back, "I'll see you tomorrow, then?"—he didn't wait for confirmation— "I better." With that, Rip crunched the bone into splinters with his powerful jaws for emphasis.

Arlo went to the exit and saw what looked like a small paver in one of the piles. He turned back to Rip with new intrigue, "Hang on? What's this?"

Rip was thrown for a loop, and the old Rip shone through as he answered with a bemused tone, "A paver?"

Arlo walked up to the small lawn mower-sized paver. "Aren't those usually massive?" He ran his paws along it with wonder. Such a simple thing that anybody ought to know, but he just didn't before now.

Rip idly tossed a splinter of bone behind him as he answered, "Sure, but not all of them."

Arlo turned back to Rip with newfound determination. This whole deal didn't have to be for nothing anymore. He exclaimed, "You know anything about that Chocolatier?"

Rip smiled. Arlo hadn't been able to keep the excitement from his voice. "You always did let the puzzle consume you, Arlo. No poker face if you show what's valuable to you." He paused and surveyed his junkyard. Then he continued, "You got your info. We can see if you get more when you actually solve my case."

Arlo was disappointed in himself. Rip was right and knew he had Arlo hooked on the line for this job. "All right. All right. I'll be back tomorrow first thing, then," Arlo said and meant it. He had considered skipping out on their deal given Rip hadn't actually provided anything, but this was a real lead potential in The Chocolatier case. He'd be back, for sure.

Chapter 7
Dreams and Realizations

Arlo walked down the street with his head held low. The pitter-patter of a Dachshund caught up to him and tried to bring him out of his stupor with her voice. "We could check the tree again."

Arlo just shook his head, "It's not there. Sally's probably home by now; you should be getting' home too. Thought you already went home."

Toots stopped walking as Arlo pressed on. She meekly said, "I wanted to make sure you were okay." Arlo didn't stop to wait for her, so she called out a little louder, "Well. See ya."

Arlo was grateful. Toots took a different route home and didn't invade his self-pity party. He approached the familiar steps of his home and saw Parker also arriving. Parker had his hands in his pockets and was deep in his own self-pity. When Arlo spotted Parker, all his sadness melted away. His tail wagged, and he raced forward to jump on Parker. The second he saw Arlo, Parker's face lit up too. It didn't matter how down they were or how tough their cases were, the partners still always had some joy for each other. Parker started the conversation to catch up, "Hey, buddy! *Ugh.* I missed ya today. Real rough one."

Arlo couldn't contain his excitement as he raced around Parker, jumping up and down. He barked, "Parker! Parker! Parker! Heck, yeah! Love! Fudge, yeah! Where were you?! I thought I'd never see you again! Today was terrible! Parker! Parker! Yeah!"

Parker just laughed and opened the door to head upstairs. "Well. Tell me all about your day, pal." He said as the two walked through the building to their apartment.

When they got inside, Parker hung up his jacket, and Arlo hung up his collar on the hat rack. Parker took his seat in front of the TV as Arlo stared at him with the largest eyes he could muster. Parker finally patted the couch to invite Arlo up, and Arlo floated directly next to Parker. He made sure to cuddle Parker to make up for the day apart. Parker must not have gotten any news on The Chocolatier case because he started with Arlo's case, "Let's go over it again. She disappears around the corner, and when she reappears, it's gone." He flipped through Arlo's notepad and went over what Arlo had found. Arlo left out his deal with Rip because he didn't want to worry Parker. Parker turned the page on the notes. "And nobody saw it happen?" Arlo nodded again, so Parker went on, "And the birds didn't see anybody else besides some park goers and Purrcella, and even the traffic footage missed the actual theft or thief?" Arlo nodded a third time before Parker finished the only way either knew he would. "Dead-end city. That's a tough one, bud. Not every case has enough, though, and I trust you did your due diligence. If this was solvable, you'd be the one to do it." Parker soothingly stroked Arlo's head and shoulders, and Arlo drifted off to sleep.

Arlo's dream was filled with a kaleidoscope of art deco buildings and the park. It all collided around him as he walked through the events of the day. Each step that Arlo took shattered the space around him into fractal colors that came back together and created a mess of a vision. Arlo found himself sniffing around the tree where Toots sat. Each bit of bark was made of feathers that shattered again and became police tape. The police tape fluttered along, becoming Toots' tail as it slowly stopped wagging and drooped to the floor. This shattered and came back together to show Toots' face. She echoed her words from earlier in the day, "It's not even worth it. It's my fault. He won't know anything."

Arlo fell off the couch as he jolted awake and exclaimed, "I know where it is!"

Parker shook off his own nap as he supported his partner, "That a boy. Where?" Parker didn't wait for the answer. He grabbed Arlo's leash and his own jacket and opened the door. Arlo threw on his collar and raced out the door, with Parker following close behind.

Arlo led Parker to the park. It was nighttime, and rats had claimed the park as theirs. The rats found every ounce of food left along the path and in the trash bins. Parker called ahead to Arlo, "Well, it's all very mysterious, my man. Wanna fill me in?" He chuckled as Arlo didn't even turn.

Arlo called back without slowing, "I couldn't find a culprit, because there isn't one."

Parker offered the simple solution, "She lost it after all."

Arlo could have kicked himself for how blind he'd been. He arrived at the tree where Toots had sat. He dug where she had sat and responded, "No. Not lost. Hidden!" With that, he uncovered the frock of a collar. The diamond was dirty, but there it was.

Parker was at a loss for words. "But… Why?"

Arlo just laughed as he fell onto his back, squirming and answering, "She hates it! Plain and simple. Look at it. It's awful. Wouldn't you? There's no perfect crime. There's just opportunity, motive, and means. It wasn't about the money. It was about the gaudiness."

Parker picked up the jabot and took a closer look at it before he rubbed Arlo's belly and offered, "Well, we should take it back to Sally then."

Parker started walking back, but Arlo bounced off his back and blocked his partner. "Hang on." Arlo said with concern, "She hates it."

Parker nodded understandingly as he stated the simple truth, "Yeah, but it's worth a lot of money. Sally's very upset—"

Arlo obstinately wouldn't give in. "Parker, you know Sally. She'll just put it back on Toots, whether she likes it or not." Parker solemnly nodded as Arlo kept barking, "It's not cool. And I like Toots. If she doesn't like it, she shouldn't have to—"

Parker put up a hand to stop Arlo. "You're right. So, what do you wanna do?"

The next morning, the two sat on the floor of the living room and played. Arlo was on his back, squirming and worming away as Parker antagonized him. Parker patted the sides of Arlo's mouth to invoke little nips and playful bites. Every few seconds, Arlo would flip around and sneeze to indicate it was just play. A knock on the door ended the play. Arlo freaked out and barked at the door. From the other side of the door, Sally's voice called out, "Would you mind watching—"

Parker mumbled to Arlo, "Here we go," as he interrupted Sally and opened the door. Then to Sally, he started right in as he pulled the diamond from his pocket, "Sally. I found the diamond, but the collar's gone. I'd recommend a safe rather than your dog's neck for something this valuable." Toots came in looking a mixture of horrified and concerned. She looked at Arlo, who just winked at her. Parker held the diamond out for Sally. "Anyways. Sorry, I didn't get the jabot back for Toots."

Sally was aghast. She launched herself forward to hug Parker. "Oh, Parker! Thank you! You have no idea how much this means to me!" She broke the hug to rifle through her purse as she babbled, "Here! Take some of it, I insist. A finder's fee or something! But I gotta go to work." She shoved a wad of cash at Parker, who just laughed and accepted it.

Parker scratched the back of his hand as he pocketed the money without looking at it. "Sure, Sal. Sure." Sally left Toots with them and went back to her apartment to deposit the diamond somewhere safer. Toots went to Arlo and nudged him gratefully with her nose. "Thanks." She said simply. They both knew what he'd done, and now that she was closer, Arlo could see she had a plain old simple collar that matched her Tootsie Roll costume a little better.

"Just doin' my job." Arlo exhaled. "Just doin' my job." Toots seemed to accept this. She went over to the corner to pee on the drapes. Arlo closed his eyes and put his thoughts on his new case. *In a city full of corruption,* He thought, *sometimes you're forced to put aside conventional ethics in order to do the right thing.* His mind drifted to where he'd be heading shortly. They'd lied to Sally—a white lie to help a friend. Where would he draw the line, though? He didn't want to go back to the life he'd lived before Parker. What was in store around the corner, working a case for a gangster?

Chapter 8
Corruption or Lies?

Arlo waited for Parker to head out for the day before he headed to Rip's. He claimed he wanted a day off after solving the last case, but Parker seemed to know better than that. Still, Parker gave Arlo the space he was asking for and left the dog alone. When Arlo exited the apartment, he called back to Toots, "I'm going for a walk. Please don't pee on my pee again while I'm gone."

He expected that to be the end of it because she never followed him out and about before, but she bounded up to his rear and cheerfully said, "You have a new case, don't you?"

"No." Arlo replied flatly as he shut the door and left.

Arlo hardly made it outside before he heard the familiar pitter-patter of Toots behind him. Toots went to his left when his head turned slightly to see more, and she caught his peripheral as she called ahead, "Okay. Let's go to the park then."

"Busy." Arlo shut her down again, but when his gaze drifted right, he found her in his peripheral again.

Toots ran up next to Arlo, so they looked directly at each other, and she stated, "So, you do have a new case."

Arlo stopped walking abruptly, which caused Toots to drift ahead. "Toots." He sounded like a worn-out fourteen-year-old dog when he spoke.

Toots wasn't having it, though. She rounded on Arlo and met him eye-to-eye. "No, Arlo. We made a good team. Yeah, I was lying to you, but we did. And I just felt—I don't know. When you went alone to see that gangster…" She paused as she gathered whatever she wanted to say next. "Whatever case you're on, I'm on. Whether you like it or not."

Arlo sighed and snorted but saw the determination in her eyes. He tried to dissuade her, "It'll be dangerous."

She walked forward again, and Arlo followed behind as she called back, "What's life without a little risk?"

Arlo caught up so they were side by side, but continued his attempts to dissuade her. "It won't all be Juise smoothies and park visits."

Toots shrugged his pessimism off. "I've been meaning to see more of the city anyway."

Arlo sighed in resignation and kept his eyes forward while they walked. He took a moment to think it over. One moment became three. When they were halfway to his destination, he accepted it had become *their* destination. He huffed out the words, "Fine. You can join me on this case, but I'm the lead detective. If I say run, you book it and don't look back. Got it?" He ended on a question, but he was certain she would agree even if she didn't mean it.

"So, there is a case." Once again, her question was more of a statement.

Arlo gave that same tired single breath of her name, "Toots."

Toots just laughed easily and replied, "Deal. So, what's the case?"

Arlo didn't like this one bit. He was walking her directly to the most dangerous dog in the city. "I dunno yet. We're gonna find out when we get there."

Toots pursued relentlessly, "Where?"

Arlo sped up his walk, so he didn't have to see her face when he admitted, "Rip's Garage."

Toots stopped. She pieced the puzzle together quickly and stated, matter of factly, "You made a deal."

Arlo didn't pause, so Toots eventually had to run to catch up. He didn't know he was still being difficult; he'd already accepted she was joining in, but he still gave a monosyllabic reply, "Yes."

Toots looked away from Arlo but kept pace as she muttered, "So it's my fault." He couldn't see her face anymore, but Arlo heard her stress panting.

"No." Arlo began, "It's…" He didn't know what to say. The truth couldn't hurt, he supposed, so he went on, "It's a long time coming. I knew him a few years ago. If it wasn't your case, it would've been another. He and I… We never settled things."

When he stopped, he could feel Toots' gaze lingering. She wanted more, but that had been enough to at least gain some silence. Arlo and Toots arrived to find Charlie and Franky in their ever-vigilant spots at the entryway. They seemed to expect Arlo's arrival as Frankly sneered, "You're late."

Charlie added, "The boss don't like being kept waitin'."

Arlo tried to ignore them, but they stopped Toots from passing by. Franky wanted answers. "Who's the broad?"

Charlie, always the original thinker, restated the question, "Who's the dame?"

Franky cocked his head to Charlie in confusion, "She ain't no Great Dane. She's a Dachshund."

Charlie snapped at Franky, his fangs biting at his ankles. His words snapped just as harshly, "Not Dane! Dame!"

Franky whined, "Well, why didn't ya say so?"

Charlie ignored Franky. He clarified their position as guards "Boss wants to see you. Not your girlfriend."

Arlo clarified for *them* all that they would need, in his opinion. "She's my partner on this case. Either she comes with me or we walk." He didn't have the option to walk. They all knew that, but it didn't matter.

Franky and Charlie looked at each other before Charlie turned to Toots. "You trust this guy?"

Toots seemed surprised at how gentle these thugs had suddenly become. Arlo wasn't surprised in the slightest. They hated him and probably felt some obligation to warn her of what a terrible dog Arlo was. Toots warily replied, "I do."

"You know what he did?" Charlie asked.

Nosy busybodies. Why was every dog Arlo knew so nosy? Of course, he was no better as a private investigator. Toots took the role of the monosyllabic as she responded, "No."

Charlie didn't let up, though. He warned, "Ask around. Find out. Smart girl wouldn't run with his type."

Toots took the bait. "Which is?"

Franky took every chance he could to talk bad about Arlo, so he jumped in. "Someone who'd stab anyone in the back for a scrap of food." Arlo shifted uncomfortably. He wanted to tell them off, but they weren't wrong. They had a right to say what they were saying.

Toots, a loyal dog, brushed them off and said, "Thanks for letting me know. Can I go through now?"

Franky and Charlie looked at her for a moment before they nodded and moved aside. Though, not without one last remark from Franky, "Keep an eye out. Back as long as yours leaves more room for gettin' stabbed in."

Arlo and Toots walked through the dark hallway back to the junkyard. Arlo wryly thought about how he hadn't been here in three years before yesterday, and now he'd been there twice in as many days. Before them, Rip was stalking back and forth and froze in an alert position when he spotted Arlo and Toots. He growled, "Who's she?"

Toots started to answer, "I'm…"

But Arlo quickly interjected, "You don't need to know who she is, Rip. I'm babysitting for the neighbor." He didn't want her anywhere near Rip's radar if he could help it.

Toots didn't make that easy for Arlo. She whipped angrily at Arlo before turning back to Rip and speaking for herself, "I'm Toots. I'm Arlo's partner on this case."

Arlo closed his eyes in irritation. Rip just looked shocked as he mused aloud rhetorically, "Partner? Wow." He looked at Arlo and said, "Parker dead weight already?"

Arlo gestured to her with his paw. "She's a new associate of Arlonius Investigations."

Rip just shrugged. "Sure. Why not?" And he hopped onto the back of the car. He lay down as Arlo and Toots stepped into the spotlight.

Arlo tried to stick to the actual issue at hand. "What's the case, Rip?"

Rip just laid his head in his paws and let the words fall out of his mouth idly, "I'm bein' set up. Those coppers out there, with their surveillance, they wanna get me for some big art deal's been goin' down." What he said sounded like a pretty large conspiracy for someone so relaxed about it.

It didn't sit right with Arlo, so he decided to press Rip. "You've never really been one for culture."

Rip smirked as he slyly replied, "Honest, Arlo. I been buying up some pieces legit. Whoever's been nabbin' these other pieces is using that—using me—to make it look like I'm just movin' in on this the same way I did some… other enterprises."

Arlo didn't let up. "And are you?" Rip growled, but Arlo wasn't done challenging this story. "Maybe you want me to prove your innocence when you aren't really. Maybe you have some poor stooge set up to take the fall, and the art mysteriously goes missing in the chaos of the actual arrest?"

Rip seemed bored with the conversation. "I've got money, Arlo. I've got power. Half the politicians in the city work for me. You know that better than most. I'm goin' straight edge. I'm movin' assets that may be a little more… suspect, but once that's all moved, it's the straight and narrow for me." He smiled an overly toothy grin.

Arlo scoffed, "Excuse me for finding that so hard to believe."

"I can't go legit?" Rip asked almost genuinely.

Arlo dismissed it, "Doubt it."

Rip replied, devoid of emotion, "You did." During this back and forth, Toots jerked her head back and forth like she was watching a soap opera, but now she paused and stared at Arlo intently. All she lacked was the popcorn for her show.

Arlo had enough of them talking about the past. The past was the past as far as he was concerned. If he needed to do one bit of detective work to leave it there, so be it. He started to leave, and Toots followed. He called back as he headed to the exit, "I'll look into it. If I get your scent on this mess, though…"

Rip just casually replied, "Hey. If you get my scent on this, I'll turn myself in." Then, he said something that caused Arlo to pause. "You got my word on that."

Arlo didn't turn as he reiterated what Rip had said as confirmation. "Your word?"

Rip took one last dig at Arlo. "Better than yours, right?"

Arlo angrily muttered, "Good enough." As he led the way out with Toots close behind.

When they were clear of Rip's Garage, Toots could hardly contain herself. "I need to know more! What happened? Were you guys partners? What'd you do? What'd he do? Tell me, tell me, tell me." Rats scuttled off into the shadows, and Arlo wished he could do the same.

Arlo spotted the humans that were tailing the dogs since they left Rip's and cryptically replied to Toots, "Maybe another time. Our ride's here."

Toots looked around in confusion, "What?"

Arlo knew they didn't have time, so he got straight to the point. "We were visiting an old friend. Got it? Nothing else." With that, they were both suddenly grabbed by humans from an alleyway, and bags were put over their heads.

Chapter 9
Getting Sick of Catching Up with Old Friends

The bag was removed from Arlo's head, and he found himself exactly where he expected to be. He was in a gray room with a mirror on the wall and a slab table with a lamp on it. He was in the city's main police station. More specifically, he was in an interrogation room. Opposite him was McMack and an older man in his fifties with jet black hair and a stiff blue uniform decorated with a plethora of medals who Arlo recognized as Chief Watanabe. Chief Watanabe held a stern expression on his always pristinely shaved face. Arlo figured they might as well get straight to it. "You two come here often?"

McMack grinned despite himself before hiding it from the Chief. Watanabe slammed his palms on the table and started with threats, "You're getting yourself involved in the middle of a police investigation. I could have you brought up for obstruction of justice!"

Arlo ignored the threats. "Don't you normally offer water to someone you've detained?"

McMack was as honest as always. "Technically, you're not actually being detained…" He shrank as Watanabe glared him down.

Arlo laughed. "So abducted? I'll be going if I'm not being detained." He stood to leave.

Watanabe didn't like that, though. He pointed at the chair and took a seat himself. The Police Chief smoothed his hair with his hands while Arlo sat back down, smiling. This was perfect. Arlo had wondered the best way to get Watanabe all worked up, and the man was practically splitting at the seams with anger already. Arlo could use this to get any information he wanted if he pushed Watanabe the right way.

"Let's start over," Watanabe said through gritted teeth, "what were you and Rip discussing?"

Arlo scratched his ear with his back leg and replied as disrespectfully as he could, "Just two old friends catching up."

McMack tried to play arbiter. "Come on, Arlo."

McMack was the only part of the equation that worried Arlo. That dog remained cool and level-headed no matter what. The opposite of the reactive Chief. Maybe if Arlo could distract him. "Where's Toots?" Arlo asked.

McMack gestured to the mirror. "She's fine. They have her in the other room."

Watanabe threw in. "She's telling my men what you and Rip talked about." Arlo could have laughed in his face. The man always liked to play cards he didn't have. Arlo knew exactly how he'd made Police Chief, but it still astounded the dog.

Arlo stood again. "Then, you know already. Just two friends catching up."

Watanabe furrowed his brow and pinched his nose as he gestured, once again, for Arlo to take a seat. The man was clearly tired. He wearily said, "Arlo. Have you really fallen so low again? I thought you'd pulled yourself out of the gutters, but here you are. Same situation. Same story. Same everything."

Arlo didn't care what the man thought, so he confirmed the man's fears. "Can't teach an old dog new tricks."

McMack stepped in again to bring in some peace. "Twice in as many days, Arlo. That's more than you've seen him in years. We just want to make sure you're still on our side is all. If he's making a move, well… if you saw anything in there. If you could give us anything that might help. You notice things quick, and none of us have gotten in there in weeks."

Arlo conceded to his friend with a half-truth, "Thought he might know something about the diamond collar case. He didn't. We buried the hatchet, and we wanted to have coffee together. Anything wrong with that?" McMack stood up and paced in the back. He was working through something. Arlo took his chance and addressed Watanabe, "You lot love your goose chases. You have nothing on me, Rip, or The Chocolatier."

Watanabe didn't hesitate to engage. He took the bait. "We have more than you'd think."

Arlo openly scoffed, "Without me doing your dirty work? Did you even know Rip was moving legit? Did you know the The Chocolatier was using a small paver and not an industrial one? Didn't think so." Arlo knew Watanabe to be a proud man. He wanted to wound that pride enough that he would let information slip.

Watanabe gritted his teeth so violently that the room echoed with the sound. "You think you're so clever." Arlo could tell McMack knew what he was doing, but it was too late, even as McMack put a paw on Watanabe's shoulder to calm him.

Arlo jabbed again. "Don't have to be to know more than you, partner."

McMack tapped the human's shoulder, but Watanabe stood in anger. "Did you know that every street that's been paved in chocolate is next to a dog park? Did you know each street had been visited by the same exterminator the week before the street was hit? Not so smart now. As for Rip going legit. he'll see the inside of a pound before I ever let that low life make a dime in his." Watanabe made air quotes, 'new ventures.' He thinks a little money laundering's gonna keep us from getting him before his little deals done and he's sitting on a corporate board of directors. He can think again."

Arlo smiled broadly as McMack exclaimed and hid his face in his paws, "Chief!" Watanabe had given Arlo a lot to work with there.

Watanabe's face turned red with anger as he realized how much he'd said, "Get out." His hand shot to point to the door, and he yelled at the small dog in front of him, "Get out of my sight!"

Arlo started walking, and despite the man's tone, Watanabe looked disappointed more than mad at the dog.

"Gladly," Arlo said. He moved past Watanabe and McMack to the exit.

Watanabe's nose twitched in anger as he said, "You won't avoid the pound this time."

Arlo felt his tone turn to steel as he tasted iron on his tongue. "Maybe. Maybe you won't avoid jail." Arlo let the door close without a glance back.

The police station was active and bustling. The room Arlo walked into quickly became a spot of whistling nonchalance as detectives and beat cops pretended they weren't watching the drama unfold through the mirror. Arlo could see some faces he recognized, but he just moved past them to open the door opposite his room's. Inside that room, Toots was speaking with two police officers. Arlo walked in as Toots exclaimed, "I told you. Catching up with an old friend."

He couldn't help but smile as he interrupted, "Come on, Toots. These dogs love chasing their tails. Best not to tell them; they'll only bite themselves." He winked as he held the door open. Toots hesitantly stood and waited for the police officers to give her the go-ahead. The officer just nodded, and Toots followed Arlo's lead.

Arlo and Toots made their way through the busy police station. Arlo led her to a doorway and stopped. He knew he was pushing it with this one, but he needed more information. He peered around the entrance to the police records room before he directed Toots, "Bark twice if anyone looks like they're coming in here."

Toots looked shocked. Arlo was certain he knew she was wondering if this was legal as she asked, "What?"

Choosing not to answer the question, Arlo thanked her quickly, "Thanks." With that, the small dog slinked into the room and left a panicked Toots, who awkwardly looked side to side.

Chapter 10
It Wasn't Legal

Arlo walked through the familiar rows of filing cabinets that made up the record rooms. He thought back to his days on the K9 unit and the hours he spent in here, which his superiors thought was a punishment. He loved nothing more than snooping through every case, open and closed, and getting his paws dirty with the mud of forbidden knowledge. He walked directly to where he knew his case of interest would be and adeptly flipped through it quickly. He started where he knew he could get a new lead on Rip and the newly recruited cadets.

Arlo took the case around Rip and brought it over to the desk with the schedules and personal information of all the officers.

Arlo thought to himself just how clever he was. He could hit two birds with one stone by following up on who in the force might know more about Rip than they were letting on and who possibly worked for Rip. He meticulously went through the names of the officers and crossed off any names that weren't within a certain proximity to Rip. Arlo knew this was a risky move because he couldn't really rule anyone out just for how close they did or didn't live to the criminal, but he had to start somewhere, and he needed to get out of the room before someone came by.

With a preliminary list of suspects from officers investigating Rip who might have more information than they let on, the small dog began the task of finding Rip's mole in the force. Chief Watanabe was a meticulous man, so Arlo had no doubt that if there was a mole, it was a cadet or a newer recruit. Watanabe would have ferreted out anyone in the force who was dirty for too long. That man would do anything to further his own career. Arlo began a new list in his notepad of suspects for Rip's mole. Rip was his client, sure, but Arlo didn't trust that dog as far as he could catch a frisbee.

Arlo froze for a moment when he heard Toots yell out in the hallway, "Oh, hey, McMack!" He raced to the next cabinet of interest. This one had the case files on The Chocolatier. Toots was clearly doing her best to buy him time. She continued talking loudly in the hallway, "Oh, nothing! I was just looking for the restroom." Arlo quickly rifled through the papers. He scribbled down the information on the exterminator and dumping sites that had already been searched throughout the city to find anything related to the case. He put together a list of dump sites they wouldn't have to double-check and the personal information of the main suspect for the police. If they had anything real on this guy, they'd have him cuffed already, but it never hurts to follow up on leads he and Parker didn't know about. Toots' voice came through the door a little more panicked this time. "What? No! Of course, Arlo wouldn't go in the file room! That would be highly illegal, I'm sure!"

Arlo's smile at what Toots was doing outside faded when he noted that no equipment had been located that showed any trace of use for paving roads with chocolate. It wasn't just this that made the dog frown; the search wasn't just for paving equipment but also equipment for growing, treating, and baking chocolate.

Arlo could have bitten himself. He realized how silly he'd been. Of course, anyone who bought that much chocolate to repurpose would get caught just for the absurd amount of chocolate they ordered. That meant this was an entire operation where someone was manufacturing huge amounts of stuff on some unknown vast site. The heat signature alone on an operation like that should have the cops down on the perpetrator's back. So, how were they hiding this much equipment in or around the city? Arlo's thoughts reeled even as he heard Toots continue to cover for him in the hallway. "Whaaaaaaaaaat! I wouldn't lie to you! I need the restroom, like I said! Here, let's go! Show me where it is." Arlo returned the files after he had the information he was looking for and decided to risk it for more information. He moved back to Rip's case files and hoped Toots could keep stalling.

Just outside the records room, Toots was practically using her long, tootsie-roll-shaped body to block McMack out of the room. The German Shepherd looked largely unimpressed by her attempts to stall him. His words were barely more than a sigh as he countered her claim of needing the restroom, "Toots. We're dogs. We pee outside."

Toots blinked as she considered the hard truth in that flat statement. She scrambled in her mind as she spoke faster than she could think, "Oh. Yeah. Silly me. The truth is…" The small dog looked up at the massive K9 unit and nervously laughed to stall further before she went on, "I was looking for…" Her eyes sought out anything in the hallway that could give her an idea, but the only thing in this beige and blue hallway was McMack, so she landed on him, "You!"

McMack reluctantly took the bait as he allowed her to stall for more time. "Why's that?"

Toots thought about how Sally used her charm to wrap any guy around her finger, and she decided to see if it could work for her. "I wanted to ask you out!" she exclaimed rather than asked.

McMack just shook his head. He didn't even entertain it as a real romantic interest. "I'm neutered. Thanks, but no thanks."

Toots' pride felt oddly hurt, despite it not being a sincere interest. She didn't let it deter her from continuing the facade of innocence. She kept on, "Married to the job, I get it. I meant… as friends!" She nervously laughed as McMack let out a chuckle, despite himself.

Arlo's search for more information had yielded unexpected results. Rip had mentioned going legit through the art world, but that wasn't his only legitimate pursuit. Buried toward the back of the dog's file, Arlo found a financial statement that declared intent to purchase enough stock in the smoothie shop, Juise, to get a seat on the board. Arlo wasn't sure it had much to do with this case, but he decided to file away that little nugget of information either way. He mused aloud, *Why is he getting in with Juise?*

His musings were cut short as he heard a far more desperate Toots from the hallway. "No seriously! Let's go grab a coffee!" As quickly as he could, Arlo tidied the room back up to what it had been before he'd entered. Better for the small dog if they didn't know exactly what information he'd gotten in here.

Back in the hallway, Toots moved side by side in an attempt to physically halt McMack from going forward. The larger dog continued to politely step to each side to go around her. She kept on with her charade. "You just seem so nice; both times now, you've dognapped me. Must be stockholm syndrome or something."

For some reason, this stopped McMack altogether, who suddenly replied in a much more serious manner, "That's not a real thing. It was invented to explain away a collective's empathy toward someone the 'psychologist' viewed as villainous. It's a term rooted, honestly, in misogyny." The dogs stopped for a moment as they considered the harm common phrases can have on society as a whole.

Then, Toots pressed on, "See. I can learn so much from you! Let's go!" Her flattery had no effect, though, because McMack had decided enough was enough. He stepped over Toots entirely. Just as he reached for the doorknob, the door opened, and Arlo walked out bold as brass. Arlo started coming face-to-face with the large dog immediately, but then sidestepped him and nudged Toots to get walking. He barely passed around McMack before declaring, "This isn't where I parked my leash. Crazy. There's a rat problem in there. You guys should get an exterminator or something." He chuckled obnoxiously at the end to try to sell the not-so-subtle lie.

When the two small dogs left, the extremely disapproving large dog, Toots, called back, "Oh, raincheck! We really should hang out outside of work, though, McMack! I really would love to! Toodaloo!" McMack just shook his head and went into the records room to see if he could find what Arlo had gotten up to in there.

Arlo and Toots crossed the street before Arlo grabbed Toots by the collar and brought her swiftly into the shadows of an alleyway. He held a paw over his mouth to indicate they needed to be quiet before he whispered, "I don't trust them; I don't trust Rip. I trust you, Toots. Even though you lied about that diamond, I trust you." Arlo hoped Toots understood the gravity of what he was saying. He wasn't one that trusted easily, but Toots had proven herself over the last three days to have an abundance of grit. Toots responded silently by nodding before Arlo went on, "I'm not going into this case for Rip blindly. First things first, we find his dog on the inside. We need to find his mole and turn them."

Arlo was relieved that Toots adopted his secrecy in the shadows immediately as she quietly responded, "Great. Let's do it. Just two questions."

"Shoot," Arlo replied.

The two dogs hugged opposite sides of the dark alleyway to blend into the shadows. Toots peered out towards the station before she returned her attention to Arlo. "What does that mean, and how?"

Arlo sighed, but she wasn't a trained detective, and he needed to remind himself of that. "Right. Okay," he said before explaining that Rip likely had a double agent on the police force who would feed him information. Arlo went on to explain how he attained the list of suspects in the records room and that they would need to spend the next week or so on stakeout. They needed to observe the police force and follow these cadets to determine who was feeding information to the gangster.

Toots held up a paw and followed up, "Okay. Can I tell Sally?"

Arlo smiled before saying, "Can't have her calling the cops about you going missing." The two dogs agreed to meet at the end of the first cadet on the list's shift. In the meantime, they both returned home to eat kibbles and nap.

That night, Arlo and Toots kept a vigilant watch on the police station. When the first cadet on the list, one Cadet, Harvey, came out the front door of the station, Arlo and Toots dogged the dog. Toots was a fast learner. She matched Arlo's speed and darted around corners whenever he did. The first night of stakeouts was incredibly uneventful. They watched Cadet Harvey return home, heat up his kibbles in some warm water to help with his digestion, and fall asleep watching wolf documentaries. Toots and Arlo weathered the cold night from across the street as they spent the night watching the cadet live an extraordinarily mundane life. They almost welcomed the presence of the rats in the alleyways when the snow started falling around them.

The next morning, the cadet went and visited a relative a few houses down the street. Arlo used Parker's detective databanks that night to figure out that it was Cadet Harvey's sister. When the cadet finished having breakfast with his sister, he went to work. All in all, the two dogs got no information out of this.

Arlo went home and checked that databank just to make sure that wasn't a contact for Rip. Then, he waited for Parker to return home. When the excited, emphatically unnecessary ritual greeting was completed, the two took their customary places on the couch in front of the TV. The two hardly talked as much as they normally would. Instead, they were both wrapped up in their own thoughts. Stakeout afternoons like this weren't new to either investigator. Both knew this was just the beginning of a very long week.

The next evening, Arlo greeted Toots with a coffee in his paw and a grimace to match. The two went back to the station and prepared themselves to repeat this process with Cadet Cally, a Border Collie who looked everything an excited young K9 unit should. With another uneventful night completed, the haze of the irregular sleep began to blend the next few repetitive days for the dogs.

The only thing that really separated the next days for the dogs as they followed Cadet Williams, Cadet Shirley, Cadet Koda, and Cadet Bodhi was the fact that Parker had to help out one of the evenings because the temperature dropped below ten degrees. The nights were cold, and the investigation was dogged as Arlo and Toots crossed off every single name from their list.

After crossing out the last name, Arlo took his notepad in his mouth and jerked it side to side like he was playing tug of war out of frustration. He dropped the notepad on the floor and thought in frustration about being pulled in every direction. Arlo was making two cases out of one and had the entire other case of The Chocolatier to worry about too. He thought how the two cases pulled him in different directions. How one of those cases was divided because he wasn't even sure of its legitimacy. This city wasn't kind to a dog searching for truth, but a grid system was supposed to be easy to understand. Arlo thought about how this city's grid felt more like a knot tied with three ropes, threatening to end up around his own neck if he wasn't careful. His musings were interrupted by Toots' voice. "That's all of them. What do we do now?"

Arlo hardly wanted to think about that, given his own spiraling. He slumped onto his butt. He sat on the sidewalk and looked out at the police station. Somehow, the station looked colder to the small dog than the weather outside. His bark was soft and muted. His hot breath hit the cold air and caused the appearance of smoke. "I don't know. It's an ongoing investigation, so they have to be in daily communication with Rip. I just don't know how…" Arlo let his own defeated voice wither into the unforgiving air.

Toots merely repeated her question as though 'I don't know' was an unacceptable response. "So what now?"

Arlo took the challenge and dared himself to stand. He replied, "We're just wasting time here. We need to start figuring out who would try to frame Rip. I've been putting together a list of suspects over the last week, but he has a lot of enemies. A lot."

Toots hopped up and confirmed what Arlo had taught her about detective work so far. "Opportunity, motive, means, right?" Arlo couldn't help but smile in surprise at how ready the Dachshund was to hop back into it after such a trial of a week.

He should have known she was also working the case in her mind on their stakeout, so he followed her lead for the moment. "Yeah? You got something?"

Toots paced as she worked through her own logic. "Well, I've been thinking. Why would someone frame him? That's the motive, but we don't know the motive. It could be as simple as revenge or as putting away a dangerous dog, right?" Toots stopped pacing and met Arlo's eyes. "But what if this is backwards? What if framing Rip isn't the motive, but the opportunity?

Arlo paused for a moment. The thought was interesting and fairly simple. Though she had said it in a somewhat convoluted manner, was someone making Rip their scapedog to get away with crimes entirely unrelated to him and only because they noticed his interest in art? "I don't know. Usually these things are more personal than…" Arlo began but was interrupted by Toots.

"Bear with me. Let's focus on the other two first. Maybe we can narrow it down that way. Then get the suspect list from there." She had a hunch, and Arlo knew that when your partner has a hunch, you back them up.

Arlo confirmed, "Okay. So, opportunity and means." The two dogs walked away from the station and went over what they knew about Rip's art theft case so far. Arlo continued, "Assuming he's innocent, the opportunity to frame Rip arose when he started moving money through the art world. This was about two weeks ago. They had to be ready to mobilize quickly. Working fast means mistakes, but they haven't made them."

Toots nodded as they walked and took the logic leap they skirted together. "So, they needed to have the opportunity already present before they knew Rip was buying up art. Also, the opportunity arose for both framer and frame-ie when The Chocolatier showed up and became the main focus of the media and the police. Making a perfect storm for the art thieves to move in quickly and quietly."

Rats scuttled around the two dogs as they walked through the alley. Arlo tried to pick up where Toots left off. "Which means…"

However, Toots was on a roll and hopped right back in. "They have the tools to break into a museum; they have the ability to go unnoticed leaving, and they have the technology or the person on the inside at each museum to…"

Arlo stopped walking as the rest of Toots' statement was drowned out by his own realization. "Wait," he said. Toots finally noticed he'd stopped and growled in curiosity. Arlo worked through the thought aloud to Toots.

"I didn't see it. None of the security teams matched up, but... I have to check something with McMack!" He could hardly form the words with the realization, and he wasn't even sure he understood it yet himself. All Arlo knew for certain was that a man on the inside really seemed to be the theme of the week. When Arlo turned to race back to the station, he ran directly into a large rat that snarled and swiped its claws at him. Arlo jumped back and barked, "Hey there! Watch it!"

The rat simply swiped at him again to make him back up further before it nastily hissed, "You're Arlo?" Arlo wasn't about to trust this strange rat who'd come out swinging, so he just tilted his head in curiosity. "Of Arlonius Investigations?" The rat went on.

Arlo asked with contention in his voice, "Who's asking?"

Toots just pushed past Arlo and put out a paw. She greeted the rat, "Yes, we're both detectives at Arlonius Investigations. How can we help?"

Arlo sulked behind her. "She's not actually licensed yet, but yeah..."

The rat pointed to a manhole in the alleyway and cryptically replied, "Mole Man wants to talk to you."

Arlo rolled his eyes and readied to pass this aggressive rat. He disregarded the gesture from the rat and said, "We're kind of busy, so you can tell this Mole Man to come by my office, and we'll try to give him a timeline on his case. We're booked right now."

The rat wasn't having that, though. It swiped again and nearly shouted, "Are you stupid? Did you think his name's actually 'Mole Man?' He's got information about your mole. He was trying to be clever about it, so you'd…" The rat threw its claws into the air in exasperation before it started to scurry away. It turned back and swished its tail to indicate 'follow.' Arlo and Toots looked at each other before they nodded and followed into the sewers.

Chapter 11
Cleaning the City Is Dirty Business

Living in a colder city had its pros and cons, and Arlo had never expected one of those cons to be climbing an extra two to four feet below the surface to get to the sewers. Arlo did his best to use the step ladder, but these things were really designed more for humans than dogs. Still, he climbed down the eight feet and landed in a squishy, squelchy puddle of disgust. It smelled like an odd mixture of coffee and feces down in these sewers. The tunnels were green and murky, with reflective light from unknown sources that bounced off of the sewage at every step. The tunnels were large and interconnected constantly, like one big mansion's hallway with doors that lead to unknown rooms and caverns.

Toots hadn't even reached the bottom of the sewer when she complained, "Maybe I should've stayed up there."

Arlo hardly had time to reply when the rat tried to hurry the two dogs along. Arlo did his best to coax Toots into the sewage. "You're telling me you faced down the biggest gangster in the city without pause, but a little dirt is too much?" Toots merely scoffed in reply as her sneer turned to grimace when her paws made contact with the floor. She turned her nose away from Arlo in protest and scrunched it in disgust from the smell of this place. The rat led the two dogs through the mess and into the dark, unknown path where this Mole Man supposedly waited.

They didn't need to travel far, as two lefts, a straightaway, and three rights gave way to the entrance and quite the surprise. The room was as open and vast as a cathedral. The ceiling was twenty or thirty feet above them, which either meant they'd traveled even lower, or this was some collapsed building forgotten by the city and left in the sewers like the rest of the city's filth. The roof had a single skylight, which showed nothing but darkness. Arlo looked around the warehouse in wonder as he pondered how this place could exist. Did another building exist on top of it? Was it just some plot of land that was fenced off and forgotten? Finally, Arlo stopped taking in the surroundings and saw the portly man in the center of the room.

The Mole Man had scraggly, unkempt facial hair and no hair on top of his head. His round glasses were covered with cracks, and he wore his plain gray coat as if he were attending a ball in a fur coat. Arlo and Toots cautiously approached the man while he stooped down, pet, and whispered to several rats, who all scurried away at the dogs' approach. The rat they had followed scurried up Mole Man's pants and through his shirt. It came out at his neckline and went onto his shoulder, where he gave it a snack of cheese. Finally, the Mole Man broke the silence. His sentences were broken, and his voice was higher pitched than Arlo thought it would be by the look of him.

Mole Man welcomed them with broad gestures and a mousy voice that didn't pair. "Welcome! Welcome! Dogs must be tired. Hope no scrape a paw on way. Sewers be," He paused while he looked up at the darkness, and the green hue of the walls bounced off his fractalized glasses onto the dogs. When the words finally came to him, he leaned in suddenly, and Arlo could see his reflection twenty or thirty times over in the glasses. "Unforgiving!" he announced and continued, "Those who no walk," He gestured side to side to show the paths and tapped his head as he leaned back out.

Arlo sarcastically replied, "With ambiance like this, how could we not enjoy the trip?"

Arlo gestured to the scenery around them and expected Mole Man to at least frown, but the man only chuckled. The man tapped his rat companion's ear and replied with good humor, "Little ears." He brought his two index fingers together and separated them in a circle as he took another moment between words, "Everywhere. Tell me, how you put it?"

Mole Man cocked his head to the side and waited for the rat to chime in. "Snarky." It replied, which caused Mole Man to chuckle again.

Arlo wasn't a fan of the pace of this conversation, so he tried to get away from the pleasantries. "And who do those ears belong to? Got a name?"

Mole Man fed the rat another piece of cheese and continued to twist and turn his head around the room, searching for words. "All belong to city, yes? All try make better." Arlo was unimpressed by the subversion from the question. Mole Man must have been able to tell this because he chuckled again and went on, "Mole Man, fine. Uppers." He indicated toward Arlo and Toots. "All think sewers dirty. But sewers clean city. Rats, we clean after uppers. Clean get." He stopped again to snap a few times as he sought another word.

His rat companion chimed in, "Associated."

Mole Man excitedly snapped and pointed up as he nodded and continued, "With dirty. We help you clean city, snarky Arlo." With that, Mole Man gently lowered the rat companion back to the ground. "Love city. Love home. Love rats."

Arlo couldn't help but roll his eyes at the prospect this guy was proposing. "So, you're an angel citizen with information to magically fall in my lap that'll help me put away criminals? Just here to do the right thing and clean up the city?" Toots put a paw on his tail while his sneer grew, and he took a breath before he returned to the best poker face he had.

Mole Man backed away as though Arlo had hurt him. "So hard believe? City can be better. All be better. This why snarky Arlo left police? Little ears always watching." Mole Man began to walk side to side as though unable to watch in a straight line. He circled the dogs while he poked and prodded with his words, "One dog want justice so much he lose all else. Even after, still does same thing before. Still investigate. Still solve crime. Still clean." He turned his attention next to Toots as he continued his interrogation of them, "Other so spoiled can't see past nose." He touched his nose just a moment before touching hers. "Now spend hours do stake out, track into sewer, information gather? Two good dog who see like me. City can be better, just need a few hands dirty to make clean."

Arlo grew increasingly more uncomfortable as Mole Man seemed to have an uncomfortably good grasp on Arlo and Toots. Arlo tried to seem like he wasn't disturbed by the depth of knowledge about their personal situations this man had. "It's a job. It pays. I trust Parker and Toots, and that's the list." Arlo couldn't help but smile as he saw Toots puff up at his words of trust.

Toots, emboldened, interjected, "And Sally."

Arlo conceded, "And Sally… but only because Toots vouches for her, and she gives really good ear scratches." Arlo paced around Mole Man this time and measured the man. He tried to glean anything he could from the man's appearance. "That said, what I don't trust is anything that falls into my lap just when I need it the most."

Mole Man chuckled again, and Arlo decided he didn't like this man's chuckle. Mole Man continued his performance as a helpful citizen, "Me? Trust easy. I give snarky Arlo Rip's." Mole Man quoted Arlo's words from the streets here and used air quotes to emphasize that fact, 'man on inside.' Like Mole said, little ears are always watching. Heard what looking for, so invite uppers down. Help." Mole Man shrugged as though this were the natural course of events.

Arlo decided to drop any pretenses. "What's in it for you?"

Mole Man seemed to grow weary of talking. "Nothing! Police focus focus focus Chocolatier. So much dirt in all other places. Rats want clean up streets. Snarky Arlo help that. Clean where police not focus, but need." Mole Man dropped into a squat and physically showed his fatigue with this conversation by jerking his head around as though he were a bored toddler.

Arlo was just as sick of this conversation and decided to bring it to an end. "All right. Let's say I believe you're an angel citizen just hoping to help. Who's his mole?"

Mole Man smiled and stopped moving altogether. He stared at Arlo. His mousy voice echoed in the halls. "Cadet Harvey."

Arlo openly scoffed at this, "We checked him already. There's no way—"

Toots interjected again. She was all business now as she questioned, "How? Like Arlo said, we checked him out. How's he getting information to Rip?"

"Oh, you follow after work. He pass words during work," Mole Man stated this as though it were obvious that a police cadet was illegally passing information in the station itself.

Toots tried to work through what this would mean. "We can't exactly follow him in the station, but Rip's people can't exactly. It doesn't make sense. Maybe there's some dirty officers, but the whole station? It's too widespread to be…"

Arlo realized how this could be done. "The cells." It made sense that somewhere a real low-time kind of dog or person could get put for an afternoon. Some petty crime, which would allow the guard to get them all the information they needed before they headed right back to Rip.

Mole Man tapped his own nose at Arlo's realization. Toots continued to work through this revelation. "So, what? He just passes information freely through the station itself."

Mole Man stood and sauntered toward the darkness at the other end of the warehouse, "No more chase own tails. Do real work now. Chocolatier get too much attention. Still other crime. Still other dirt need clean." His voice carried just long enough to see him disappear into the shadows.

Arlo and Toots walked alone back the way they came. Arlo looked over his shoulders a few times to make sure they weren't followed before he said, "I don't like it."

Arlo studied Toots' face. She seemed to agree with him despite her words, "It makes sense."

Arlo shook his head and agreed, "Oh, I'm sure it's true. It fits too nicely not to be."

Toots looked at him with curiosity. "Then what?"

Arlo couldn't figure out Mole Man's angle. What was the missing piece of why he volunteered this information? He posed the question to Toots. "Nobody offers something for nothing. What does he get out of this?"

Toots optimistically proposed, "Maybe he really just wants to help?"

Arlo couldn't help but shoot that down. "No… Not that one. He's watching too closely. That thing he said about chasing our own tails? I said that. About the police. And the other thing—"

Toots sighed. She finished the thought, "He literally put your man on the inside in quotes. I remember. Yeah, it was a little ominous, but—"

Arlo interjected as though they had shared the thought that brought them there. "Toots. What do you think? Really? You read people better than me."

Toots paused and forced Arlo to follow suit. She puffed up again. "I think we follow the information we have and worry about him when we know more." Arlo sighed, nodded, and pulled himself up the ladder while they exited the sewer.

Chapter 12
Mole to Mole to Mole

When Arlo and Toots arrived back across the street from the police station, Arlo made up his mind quickly about what to do next. Toots asked Arlo, "What's the plan?"

Arlo looked toward the police station and waited a moment before he saw Chief Watanabe and McMack as they idled about outside. He turned to Toots. "If it was just McMack, I'd just ask him to put me in the cells for a bit."

Toots' eyes wandered back to the station before she replied, "The Police Chief is with him."

Arlo smirked and went on, "Yeah. Change of plans. You wait here." Arlo walked directly across the street to the two officers with purpose. He left Toots behind. Arlo knew exactly how to get an afternoon in the cells.

McMack's tail wagged upon seeing his friend. He exclaimed, "Arlo! Here again, so soon! You must really be on the case if you…" However, McMack was quickly cut short. Arlo bit at the German Shepherd's heels. Watanabe didn't hesitate for a moment; he just sighed and quickly cuffed Arlo's paws. Arlo could hear the hurt in McMack's voice. "Arlo?"

Arlo hardly had time to reply while Watanabe dragged him into the station. "Guess I'm just a bad dog. Sorry,

McMack." Arlo frowned while he watched his friend lick his heels in confusion and hurt. He only looked away when Watanabe grabbed him by the scruff of his neck and carried him into the station's cells. Watanabe threw Arlo into the cells. The room looked as it always did, lined with jail cells and barren of any semblance of dogmanity.

Watanabe threw Arlo in the largest cell with a few other people and dogs in it that seemed to be sleeping off the night before. Watanabe's barely moved as the questions tumbled out of his tight-lipped mouth, "Well, you probably got what you wanted. Assaulting a police officer? What were you thinking, Arlo?"

Arlo just sneered at his former partner, "Once a bad dog, always a bad dog, Watanabe." With that, Arlo circled around the cold ground and laid down in a donut shape.

Watanabe stood there for a moment before he sighed and shook his head. McMack entered just long enough for Watanabe to walk past him. "I'm not the only one that wants to help you, Arlo. It may not seem like it, but the Chief still thinks highly of you. You know you can trust me, right?" Arlo could tell, even now, McMack assumed Arlo had the best intentions. Arlo tried to grimace at that fact.

Arlo lifted his head to acknowledge the K9, "Are you hurt?" McMack lifted his paw and shook his head. Arlo put his head back down and looked away until he heard McMack exit. Now all the small dog had to do was wait for Cadet Harvey to be on duty.

A few hours passed before Cadet Harvey walked in to relieve the dog before him, who stood guard over the cells.

Cadet Harvey wore his vest much more casually than McMack. The vest was open and hung near the ground. When Cadet Harvey took a seat, Arlo walked up to the cell bars and stared at the corrupt officer. He stared until Harvey took notice and called, "What are you looking at, prisoner?"

Arlo squinted like he was really trying to take the whole picture in before he casually replied, "Rip used to be better at picking them."

Cadet Harvey bolted upright before he looked around wildly and anxiously. He bolted over to the cell from his dog bed behind his desk and whispered urgently, "Hey! Watch your mouth, prisoner!" Without waiting for a reply, Cadet Harvey used his mouth to pull a baton from his vest.

He used the baton to rap the cells before he dropped it and whispered again, "What are you playing at, scum?" Arlo almost broke into laughter at this odd display. This dog clearly didn't know how to keep its cool. Cadet Harvey continued, "I thought Rip wasn't sending anyone until tomorrow? Did something happen?"

Arlo gestured for Cadet Harvey to lean in, which the cadet did. Arlo grabbed at the cadet's loose vest with his teeth and tore it. In the process, he pulled Cadet Harvey hard against the bars. Arlo smiled wickedly and said to the corrupt cop, "You keep this zipped, so you don't have loose clothes. Makes for something easier to grab. Also, it leaves you vulnerable." Cadet Harvey yelped and scrambled to back up, but Arlo made sure not to lose his grip on the vest while he talked with his mouth full. "You're gonna have to be more careful if you want to last.

Be smarter, and don't fall for everything you hear right away, kid."

Arlo tossed the cadet back. Cadet Harvey scowled while his neck hair bristled at the small private investigator. "What are you playing at?"

Arlo ignored the question and went on his own tangent, "So, you're Rip's mole in the force."

Arlo shook his head in disappointment. "I know Rip's angle. What's yours?"

Cadet Harvey got increasingly agitated. "Keep your voice down!"

Arlo looked around at the sleeping slobs in the same cell as him. He raised his eyebrow and challenged the cadet, "Why?"

Cadet Harvey came closer but stayed far enough that Arlo wouldn't be able to reach him again. "What if someone hears?"

Arlo just laughed and asserted, "Listen carefully, Cadet. You're my dog on the inside now. Anything you bring, Rip, you bring me first."

Cadet Harvey looked shaken. He finally began to grasp the situation. "You're not here for Rip."

Arlo rolled his eyes. "You catch on quick. I'm a private investigator."

Cadet Harvey zipped his vest up and smoothed it out as though physically recomposing himself. "Well. Newsflash. I'm more scared of Rip than some mutt P.I."

Arlo looked at the pup and weighed his next words carefully. He considered what this young pup might have heard about him from either Rip or from someone in the force itself. Arlo considered how his reputation had grown to something of a myth outside of Rip's immediate circle. The only dog to stab Rip in the back and not wake up with a fang in their own back. Arlo wondered if he could use that here, so he pushed his snout through the cells and tested the waters. "Name's Arlo."

Sure enough, Cadet Harvey's posture stiffened, and he seemed to have some notion of Arlo as a boogeydog. "Arlo? As in…" He paused as his eyes widened. "Is it… true?"

Arlo smirked; he had the fish on the bait. "Yeah." Of course, Arlo had no idea what this dog thought or what he was asking. But Arlo didn't really care either.

Cadet Harvey looked torn as his eyes flitted side to side. "What if Rip catches me?"

He looked up at Arlo, and Arlo could tell he wasn't really refusing. He was looking for an excuse to give in to Arlo's will. "You let me deal with Rip. Now what do you have?"

Cadet Harvey seemed to lower his head as he submitted, "Nothing! Nothing new's come through, and no word of a new score."

Arlo continued with more confidence, "All right. Tell me what you already told him." He wondered if he should act like he knew more than he did, so he added a little spice to this cooked dish. "I'm testing you, cadet. Lie to me, and I'll know."

Cadet Harvey seemed intent on proving any bluff useful. He gave everything he had over immediately. "Right. Just what I told Rip. Intel came in from an unknown telephone source three days before the art was stolen that Rip was gathering a team to rob the place. Didn't matter. The score happened right under the police's noses each time. This happened three times. Same thing each time. Different places, different security companies, different everything. No new calls have come in."

Cadet Harvey stopped talking the moment the door behind him opened. McMack walked in and announced, "Arlo. You made bail."

Arlo was visibly upset as Cadet Harvey opened the cell door and let Arlo out. When he passed the cadet, he whispered, "Remember. You come to me first next time anything comes up."

Arlo wanted to apologize as McMack led him to the front of the station, but he couldn't work up the courage. Arlo scoffed at himself. He thought about all the dangerous animals, situations, and positions he put himself in. He could face that with no hesitation, but apologizing to his friend seemed Herculean in comparison. At the entrance of the station stood Parker. Parker just smiled at Arlo and put the dog's leash on him. "Get anything good, at least?"

Arlo gave a toothy grin. "We have a lot." Maybe apologizing to McMack was hard, but Parker always seemed to understand Arlo. They didn't always see eye to eye on everything, but they always gave the other the benefit of the doubt. That was part of why Arlo trusted Parker more than anyone else in the world.

Parker smiled and confirmed he'd been no slouch about their work on his end either. "Same here."

Chapter 13
This Whole Case Is Suspect

Arlo and Parker returned to their apartment, and Parker plopped into his usual spot on the couch. Immediately, Arlo, ever the good dog, did circles at Parker's feet until Parker patted the couch to invite him up. When Arlo leapt onto the couch, it looked more like he levitated as he landed perfectly next to the affectionate Parker.

Parker put his face right in Arlo's and ruffled the top of his head as he exclaimed, "Can I go first?" Without waiting for a reply, Parker went on, "I found the dump site! Just like you said, I stopped looking for a large commercial paver. There are several personal pavers with chocolate residue in the north side dump." Arlo licked Parker's face excitedly. They both had good news to share. "That's not all! I gave the tip to the cops, and we're officially on the case as consultants!" At this news, Arlo hopped up and down before jumping off the couch. Arlo raced into the office to get to work, leaving a somewhat put-out Parker on the couch. "Really? Can't we just…" Parker sighed when he realized his pleas for relaxation would fall on deaf ears. Parker relented, slapped his thighs to motivate himself, and stood to follow. "You know, most jobs have ten or fifteen minute breaks now and again! Pretty sure they legally have to!" Parker yelled louder than he needed while he walked into the office.

Before he even walked three steps, Arlo replied from the office, "Most jobs don't have the thrill of the hunt!"

Parker chuckled and meandered slowly into the office to find Arlo. He was already hard at work updating the corkboard on Parker's side of the office. Parker walked over to Arlo's corkboard and just looked at it thoughtfully. Arlo was more than happy to jump right in. "All right! Let's start from the top! What we know and what we don't."

However, Arlo was interrupted by the front door opening and closing. This sent Arlo into a frenzy. He raced toward the door, barking his head off. He was cut off, though, by a glaring Toots standing in the doorway. She barked sharply in his face, causing him to turn and tuck his tail. "What were you thinking? Do you know how worried I was?" Arlo tried to slink away, and Parker just laughed at the unfortunate dog. Toots reeled at the laughing human, "And you! You were supposed to bring me to get him!"

Parker stammered out any response he could, "I... sorry. I just..."

Toots wasn't having it, though. She calmed down with a deep breath and dismissed the poor behavior by both parties in front of her. "Never mind all that!" She turned back to Arlo. "Did you talk to Harvey?"

Arlo gestured to Parker and the smaller of the two corkboards. "I was just getting to that with Parker."

Toots waited, while Arlo and Parker both looked like deer in headlights as they sought out whether to continue or not. Finally, Toots exclaimed, "Well. Get to it, then. We're all here."

Parker hopped in and walked over to the larger of the two corkboards, "Let's start with The Chocolatier."

Arlo joined him at his side and pointed to the circled dump site on the city map. "We have the means. These small pavers. We still don't have where the chocolate comes from or how they're getting these pavers to begin with."

Parker connected some string from the dump site to several other dumps around the city, "Well, I was able to track down the original owners of all the pavers. They were all junked. Scrapped for parts and thrown away."

Toots walked over and observed the two detectives lining up their facts and connections. She asked, "But they still worked for The Chocolatier? Does that mean they're fixing them up?"

Parker backed away from the board as he put his hand to his chin and mused aloud, "I thought that at first, but I think they're junked in pretty good condition. Whoever's doing this has been planning this for a while. The chocolate operation, the pavers, they had to be collecting this stuff over years."

Arlo backed up to match his partner and began, "Okay. So that's part of the picture."

Toots, however, stepped forward as she pivoted to her own thought. "We also have the opportunity. So, all we're missing is the motive."

Arlo stepped alongside Toots and questioned her assertion, "We do?"

Toots slapped up a picture of Rip. Then, she took a string and connected the two corkboards from across the room. She led a string from Rip to the mystery framer in Arlo's case. Then she explained, "What if it's not just the guys who are framing Rip using Rip and The Chocolatier as distraction? What if all three of them are doing it? Rip's making a move into legitimate business, the thieves framing him use him, but so could The Chocolatier. With the police being spread thin, it creates an opportunity for them too. We've been assuming the art thieves are using The Chocolatier, but what if they're using one another. Like a crime wave."

Parker traced his finger along the string. He looked from conspiracy board to conspiracy board and how they connected. "So, under that theory, The Chocolatier's just been waiting in the shadows for something big enough to distract the cops, but he'd need to know already that the art thieves were also waiting on some opportunity," he said.

Toots continued her line of logic, "Think about it, with full-time surveillance on Rip. Maybe the police aren't equipped to watch the whole city right now."

Arlo thought it was a bit of a leap, but he was willing to follow it to its conclusion. "If that's true," he stated, "The Chocolatier would want to make sure the police stay distracted, and they'd be working toward something, not just randomly hitting streets like we thought. What if we've met The Chocolatier already?" Arlo was working through this himself, but he felt confident that if Toots' hypothesis was correct, then The Chocolatier would do anything they could to keep the cops on the tail of the art thieves and off their own.

Parker and Toots both waited as Arlo paced from side of the office to side of the office and took in both corkboards. "So? Out with it!" Toots wasn't having any of his shenanigans today, not after she saw him get arrested.

Parker tried a more soothing approach to break through Arlo's quiet thought process. "Who do you have in mind?"

Arlo stopped and looked at his partners. "I'm not totally sure, but I have some suspicions. We need to lay a trap."

Parker nodded. "Any ideas?"

Arlo was shocked at Toots' suggestion, "What if we use Sally's diamond?" she offered. "Loan it to the museum and do a whole event for it?" It was startling to the small dog to hear Toots volunteer something of her and Sally's wealth as bait. It would help to control the night that they needed to act. It would also remove any unnecessary guesswork about what the best night to hit the museum would be for the art thieves, therefore giving the opportunity for The Chocolatier to hit the cul-de-sac. Still, it was risky to use such a family heirloom as bait.

Arlo decided he'd given her the benefit of the doubt this far. If her assertions were right, they could get both criminals in the same night. "Perfect, then maybe. Just maybe. The Chocolatier will come to us," he agreed with Toots' idea.

Parker was less on board. "Then that just opens us up to the art thieves. While we're focusing on The

Chocolatier, they get the diamond and whatever else they want."

Arlo considered this a moment, but he was ready for that objection, "That. I had an idea about that after talking with Cadet Harvey." Toots rolled her eyes as Arlo paced again.

Parker was less patient this time. He gave Arlo the command he'd taught him earlier that year. "Arlo. Speak."

Arlo shook out of his daydream about the case to explain his thought process. "Sorry. The security guards."

Parker didn't follow yet as he challenged, "They looked into that. None of the companies on security for the museums match, and none of them had employees that crossed over between companies either."

Arlo knew that. He also knew what he was about to say would likely be the most dangerous line of thought this case had seen. "Right. Cadet Harvey got me thinking, though. What if he's not the only dirty cop?"

Parker warned, "That's a dangerous thread to walk, Arlo."

Arlo tried to stay calm while he worked through the thought he'd been having since speaking with Cadet Harvey. "But listen, it makes sense. What if there's a couple or even several officers? They'd show up to the scene, not find anything and make off with the art."

Toots seemed to humor the idea. "That's all well and good as a theory, but it doesn't explain how they get anything past security to begin with."

Parker walked over to his desk and snapped his fingers with realization. He pulled out a packet of documents and scrolled through them. "Maybe it does." While he said this, he opened the pages to the security company's list of employees. "Look. It's not uncommon for police officers to moonlight private security." He pulled out another sheet of paper from his desk in a drawer. Then, he pointed to them both and said, "See? Already!" Arlo looked over his shoulder to see that he was pointing to matching names between an officer and a security guard who had worked at one of the museums that was hit. "Arlo. Can you get me that new cadet list? I want to make sure I have the full list of officers."

Arlo handed Parker the note from his pad. Then, he walked over to the larger of the two corkboards to focus on The Chocolatier while Parker focused on the art thieves. "Then I have one more thing for The Chocolatier case," Arlo announced.

Toots offered the information before Arlo had a chance to say, "The exterminator?"

Arlo confirmed, "Exactly. The cops haven't released this fact because it's their main lead. There's an exterminator that's gone out to each cul-de-sac hit just a day or two before each chocolate paving."

Parker scribbled some names down on a piece of paper as he yelled, "Got it!" He walked over to Arlo's corkboard and slapped up a list of four names. "Then these are our suspects here for who's framing Rip."

Arlo went back toward his desk while he tried to contain his excitement. "So, we have new leads." At his desk, Arlo pulled a phone out of his drawer. The phone was a landline with massive buttons suitable for a dog's paw to hit.

Parker grabbed his jacket and didn't seem to notice what Arlo was doing. "Let's hit it then."

Arlo called after Parker when he left the room for the front door, "I'll be right there. I'm gonna have Cadet Harvey follow up on these names for me." As the phone rang, Arlo couldn't help but be excited. Things were finally going their way in these cases, and they had leads on all fronts. Arlo could feel the truth just out of reach. The puzzles were unraveling, but it still felt like something was wrong. This city had a way of making highs low and lows high when least expected, and Arlo was all too familiar with that fact. Still, he relayed the names to Cadet Harvey quickly and hung up on the confused German Shepherd. With that in the works, Arlo rushed after Toots and Parker and met them at the car. Toots had apparently already called shotgun, which meant Arlo sat in the back seat. In the car, he leaned forward through the center, trying to nudge his way onto Parker's lap. Parker continuously pushed him back, much to Arlo's distress. However, Arlo wasn't one to give up, so he whined and pleaded the whole way to the exterminator's office.

When they arrived, they found a hut-like building outside of a much larger shed all fenced in. The shed had open doors and loads of equipment including tarps, masks, and other necessities for exterminating vermin and bugs. Parker went up to the office and knocked while Arlo and Toots walked around the building sniffing air and ground.

With no answer, Parker got suspicious. "Something's not right."

Arlo looked around the other side of the small hut and saw a car in the lot. "His car's here," Arlo relayed to the others.

Toots had her nose in the air and grimaced as she questioned, "What's that smell, though?"

Parker knocked a third time and called out, "Mr. Luthor?" He tried the door, only to discover it was open. That made sense; it was a business after all. Why wouldn't it be open to walk-ins? Something was still off, though. Parker called into the office, "You guys open?"

Parker, Arlo, and Toots cautiously entered the little shack. The office had a plain little kitchen with a table and a few chairs. There in the kitchen, next to the microwave, was the computer for actual business. It was clear to Arlo that not a lot of work was done here. They walked in, and the back door slammed shut in front of them. Arlo wondered for a moment why it was open at all.

Toots approached the table and sniffed the tea. There was worry in her voice. "Arlo?"

Arlo stopped abruptly when he saw it. Behind the table's dinner cloth on the ground was the shape of a man slumped over. The small dog didn't waste any time as he rushed to Mr. Luthor's side to see if he was still alive. "Parker. Call an ambulance. Now." Arlo told Parker to do this because he knew that in emergency situations it was always important to single out one person to call 911. Inaction could often be the largest problem in these situations, and when you single someone out, it assigns responsibility and avoids chaos. Arlo held a pocket mirror to Mr. Luthor's mouth and found he was still breathing. While Parker called 911, Arlo looked for a cause of this man's situation. The man had fallen and knocked his head so he was unconscious. Arlo couldn't find any sign of a struggle, though.

Toots gave Arlo that reason, "Arlo. It's rat poison."

Arlo looked at the tea Toots was sniffing then back to the man struggling to survive. "Then he's…" Arlo realized what this meant. The back door hadn't slammed because of the wind. Someone had been here. Someone had done this!

Arlo put the man down for hardly even a second when Parker yelled at him, "Arlo! We don't have time to chase this guy! You know what to do!" Parker spoke clearly and directly into the phone, "Hi, yes, my name is Parker, and I need poison control at…"

Arlo looked at the back door, still flapping open and closing in the wind, before he shook it off to remain at Mr. Luthor's side. He needed to get this man a drink of water. Toots was in a panic, and she asked, "What do we do? What do we do? Do we make him throw up? Where are the carrots?"

Arlo knew enough about poison control procedure that vomiting shouldn't be induced unless an expert tells you to. "No," he responded. "Not unless poison control tells us to. He likely had a muscle spasm from the poison and fell over. For now, we just prop him up and try to get him to drink water. All we can do is wait on the experts to arrive." Toots nodded in understanding, and positioned herself behind the man so Arlo could push him upright. Arlo tipped some water into the man's mouth, but stopped when he could tell the man wouldn't be able to drink it on his own. Arlo felt powerless. He considered the still flapping door in front of him. He knew this wasn't an accident. This was The Chocolatier, and they'd stepped it up to attempted murder.

Chapter 14
But, Like, What's Your Actual Name?

The next few hours were a blur. The ambulance arrived first with McMack on their tail. The catty E.M.T.s were chatty as they brought this guy back from the brink of death. McMack spent a good hour with Parker and Arlo to get the story numerous times. Eventually, McMack decided he'd send a police escort with the exterminator to recover in a hospital, then it'd be off to police custody for protection services in some safe house until they could learn more.

None of that mattered to the private investigators; things had escalated here. The Chocolatier wasn't just paving the streets with sweets. They were poisoning people.

Watanabe was furious when he showed up. He was convinced Arlo had tipped off the prime suspect that he was a suspect, and this whole thing was an elaborate set-up. As far as Arlo was concerned, a man could twist any story to make Arlo the bad dog. Everything else was a blur after such a horrific event. Arlo didn't even remember when Watanabe stopped yelling at him and let the investigators leave the scene.

Finally, Parker, Arlo, and Toots returned home. However, it was clear Arlo wouldn't be getting rest anytime soon. Outside, they were stopped by a familiar rat. Arlo nodded Parker on. "You go ahead. I gotta go dig through some trash."

Parker looked at the rat before responding, "Sure, you don't want me coming with you? Six r paws are better than four." It was clear to Arlo that Parker was concerned about the timing, the same as he was. Right after an attempted murder, Mole Man reaches back out.

Arlo tried to play it off casually. "Nah, I think I'm visiting a guy who considers himself something of a janitor. Should be pretty clean." Arlo followed the rat into a manhole. They traveled through the twists and turns of the underground canals. Taking a different route, they found the same destination. The vast warehouse underground became a meeting place for Arlo and the Mole Man yet again. What Mole Man didn't know was that by calling Arlo down here, he had become suspect number one in the case of The Chocolatier.

"Little ears," the Mole Man began, "got news for snarky Arlo."

Arlo breathed in and out steadily. He prepared himself for this game of chess. He had suspicions, but he'd been wrong about suspects a number of times this week alone. He considered how convinced he'd been that Purrcella was the perpetrator of the jabot case. He needed some sort of confirmation, and he intended to get it in this conversation. "Oh, yeah?"

Mole Man seemed all too happy to carry on the conversation at the moment, as the familiar over-gesticulation began while he spoke, "Big time. Art gon' move five-day time. Big diamond event. Big score, big theft, big chance for snarky Arlo and police." Mole Man nodded as he spoke, like this was the most exciting news he could offer. "Here—" he went on as he tucked a packet of documents into Arlo's collar.

Arlo gave the Mole Man some serious side eye at how familiar he'd grown. He asked, "What's this?"

Mole Man smiled. "Them's crooked cops. Each one." He looked around as though cautious, wondering who might overhear. Arlo was even more convinced it was all an act. "Work different security. Organize so never same company, never same officer. Big scheme."

Arlo had come to that same conclusion with Parker, but it never helped to show his hand to an opponent, so he challenged instead, "That's quite an allegation." He looked around and smelled the air before laying it on thickly. "I really admire your dedication to this city, Mole Man. Maybe the sewers aren't that bad. Now that I think about it, they kinda smell sweet. A little bitter, but sweet. Like coffee." Here was his first real challenge to Mole Man. He brought up the smell of coffee purposefully because cocoa had another thing it made besides coffee. It also made chocolate.

The Mole Man shifted; he looked visibly uncomfortable under the scrutiny of Arlo. "Never know what come down these parts. Uppers keeps us on toes, this true."

Arlo casually paced around the room, making a point to peer down each tunnel. This guy was careful, with a lot of exits and none obviously leading anywhere helpful. Arlo wondered if one of these tunnels might lead to a similar opening as the one here. A warehouse big enough for a full cocoa-growing operation beneath the city, hidden and producing enough chocolate to pave street after street, "Well, if you want credit for the help you're giving this city, go ahead and come on out into the light when we catch these guys. You'll be watching from the sewers, right?" Arlo pretended to change the subject.

"Me? Nah, rats no in it for glory. Just make city better place." Mole Man shrugged off the suggestion with practiced humility.

Arlo had skirted the topic, but he wanted to really throw Mole Man off to get a reaction. "Oh, hey, before I go. Since you've been so helpful on this. Have you heard anything about that Chocolatier?" He posed the question as an afterthought in the hopes he wouldn't scare Mole Man off, but looked for the reaction.

"Nothing come through little ears." Mole Man tilted his head left and right, up and down. He spoke carefully, "Chocolate none poison rats like does dogs. Don't pay much attention, Chocolatier. Police and snarky Arlo better off pay more attention to threats Mole Man *can* help with. Yes?" His smile looked forced to Arlo.

Arlo didn't relent quite yet. "Funny. So altruistic about the art thieves, but not so much about the chocolate."

Mole Man shrugged. "No control what little ears hear. Might just be they like scraps of chocolate." He posed it as a joke, but Arlo didn't laugh.

Arlo didn't want to push it too far, but it was time to dive in. "Yeah. Funny how someone up there's really replacing poison for rats with poison for dogs."

Mole Man hung his head low and shook it side to side as he said sorrowfully, "Nothin' funny 'bout poison, you ask me."

Arlo couldn't help but feel like Mole Man was being sincere with this statement. "Yeah, well, if you hear anything."

"Snarky Arlo first dog to know," Mole Man finished Arlo's sentence. Arlo decided not to push this further into enemy territory, so he started to leave. Mole Man didn't let it lie though, as he called out, "Hang on. One my little ears show you way."

Arlo didn't bother to pause as he went, "That's all right. I'm getting a good idea of these sewers. Might even spend some time looking around." He didn't look back, but he listened keenly to hear any worry in Mole Man's voice.

"Sure sure. Don't get hurt now. No help down here." Mole Man's voice was level, but that seemed like a threat to the neurotic small dog. He wanted to throw the Mole Man off, but it didn't seem to work. Arlo began to rethink how it had played out. Maybe he'd laid it on too thick; he didn't want to scare him off after all. Still, Arlo had no doubts in his mind. After that conversation, Mole Man was The Chocolatier. Arlo just needed the proof.

These thoughts consumed him all the way back to his doorstep. Once more, Arlo was stopped short. He wondered if he was ever going to get some rest. This time, it was Cadet Harvey who grabbed Arlo from the shadows. Arlo looked him up and down. He didn't think he'd scared Mole Man off, but something sure had scared Cadet Harvey by the looks of him.

Cadet Harvey urgently spilled and tumbled his words, "*Psst.* I gotta go, man. I gotta go. I looked into those names you wanted me to, and man. I'm in over my head. I got a sister at home who doesn't have anyone else. Between you, Rip, and the cops. I'm out, man. I'm out. You're barking up the right tree, but I think it's getting cut down. I don't wanna be under it when it falls. I'll say this much. Rip's being set up."

Arlo absentmindedly made sure the documents from Mole Man were still tucked safely in his collar as he replied, "You know who?"

Cadet Harvey threw a piece of paper on the ground as he backed away. "I can't, man. I can't. I gotta go."

Before Arlo could say another thing, Cadet Harvey was gone. Arlo looked at the piece of paper on the ground; it had the names of four officers. He pulled the packet of documents from his collar and opened it. Sure enough, it was the same list of officers with more detail on their day-to-day movements. Mole Man's little ears were thorough; Arlo could hardly keep from laughing. He'd gotten two independent sources to give him the same crooked cops. Arlo couldn't help but wonder if Watanabe had become what he'd hated so much. After all, how could the man running the precinct not realize what was going on under his nose? Arlo decided he needed to dig more, but he wanted Cadet Harvey to calm down.

So, Arlo decided to wait a day or two to visit Cadet Harvey's apartment. An impatient dog, Arlo, ended up only waiting for the day. It was too late; Cadet Harvey's apartment was empty, and he'd skipped town. He wasn't just scared; he was terrified. With all the pieces set in motion.

It was time to gamble on trust. Parker, Toots, and McMack. The list wasn't long, but Arlo had to trust them. If he couldn't gather more information, he needed to create some. Arlo decided it was time to strike.

Chapter 15
Who Do You Trust?

Arlo sent the word out with the help of Parker and Toots. They needed a neutral place to meet and bring everyone involved together to come up with a real plan to catch two different groups of criminals. One was The Chocolatier, and the other was a group of crooked cops who were stealing art and framing Rip. None of this was pretty, and Arlo couldn't imagine a scenario where at least a few disputes didn't break out. Arlo considered carefully where to meet but landed quickly on Ruff's Tavern. The worn-out, rough-around the edges bar with stools and booths was the perfect quiet place where they could all meet without much notice.

When Arlo arrived at his familiar joint, he sneezed. The place wasn't nice, and there was dust everywhere except for a dozen or so of the seats. This place survived on its regulars. Arlo and Parker sat down at the bar to try to come up with a game plan for keeping things civil, while Sally and Toots went to a booth for the whole group. Larry, Jerry, and Terry arrived first, and Arlo sent them on their way to the booth. He shook his head at how Toots had clung to these birds as reliable. He didn't agree, but he didn't have a good reason not to seek their help. The next arrival was Rip. Parker finished his apple juice and walked with Rip back to the booth, leaving Arlo alone at the bar. Finally, Watanabe and McMack entered the bar. That was everyone.

Rather than sending him on to the booth, Arlo gestured for Watanabe to join him at the bar. Chief Watanabe hung his coat at the doorway. Toots waved McMack down, but he paused a moment, looking at the stiff Watanabe standing next to a seated Arlo. McMack grimaced but left the two alone.

Arlo pulled the chair out without looking up at Watanabe, but the Police Chief didn't take a seat. Instead, he scowled at the dog, "What did you want? Trying to get a public nuisance collar this time?" Watanabe gestured toward Arlo's brown drink.

Arlo just rolled his eyes and held up his drink. "It's apple juice. Just sit down. We need to talk." He didn't like this any more than the Chief seemed to.

Watanabe was stubborn as ever, and he pressed his point. "This looks an awful lot like a set-up to me. City's most notorious gangster sitting with the Chief of Police. This a photo op?" Arlo could tell from his peripherals that Watanabe was scanning the place for a camera hidden somewhere.

Arlo just pushed the chair further out as he sighed. "Let's get things straight between us before we go sit with the others."

Watanabe finally relented and took a seat as he asked, "What's there to get?"

Arlo wanted to move through this conversation as quickly as he could. So, he jumped right in, "What happened's in the past." Arlo could practically feel Watanabe roll his eyes and move to leave. So, Arlo put his paw on Watanabe's arm and continued, "We used to trust each other." He knew it was a nothing statement. With trust being broken, how could they move forward just by acknowledging it?

Watanabe accused, "That was before I saw who you really were. Now get off of me; I'm the Chief of Police, and you'd put a paw on me." The man challenged his former partner. Arlo did nothing but slide a drink in front of Watanabe.

"Just sit down." Arlo wearily pleaded. Watanabe looked down at the paw, over to McMack, and eventually picked up the drink and tossed it back before sitting. Arlo tried to explain without justification. There was no reason to get into who was right and who was wrong in the past. If they were going to be able to work together here and now, that needed to be put behind them. "What happened happened. We've both moved on, and we're both different than we used to be."

Watanabe pointedly looked at Rip before he dismissed Arlo's point, "Looks about the same to me."

Arlo nodded. "I know how it looks," he began. "I'll explain why Rip's here when we go sit down. He has nothing to do with…"

Arlo managed to hit a nerve without even meaning to this time. Watanabe broke in angrily, "You were dirty! Rip's the one that turned you! Now you expect me to just go sit and chat with you both? Now you're saying forget. Forget, forget what happened? You can justify it to yourself all you want, but you're a bad dog, and I'm the Chief of Police. I can't—"

Arlo didn't mean to, but he ended up slamming his glass down on the bar counter, "Fine, you don't trust me. I don't trust you either." Arlo stopped himself and drank his apple juice before he put the glass down carefully this time. He slid the papers over to Watanabe. "If you don't wanna hear what I have to say over there, fine. Here's the information you'll need to put away the real art thieves. All that's missing is the hard evidence, which I'm getting shortly." He could make fun of Watanabe all he wanted for that short temper, but Arlo knew the hurt went both ways, and he was just as quick to rise because of it.

Watanabe flipped through the pages and laughed before tossing them back down. "You can't be serious." He spat his words at Arlo, "Who told you this nonsense?"

Arlo readied himself for an onslaught of accusations. He knew how what he was about to say would sound. Still, he had to say it. "I think." He paused just a moment. "I think The Chocolatier told me." He rushed through the last words to get them out quickly and be done with it.

Watanabe held up a finger for the bar tender to get him another drink. "All right. You have my attention."

Arlo was shocked, but went on, "I don't know where they hide the goods, but I know when they're hitting the next museum. We set that up ourselves."

Watanabe sipped his drink and laughed with a mixture of confusion and realization. "You set up the event? But the diamond? They wouldn't be stupid enough—"

Arlo cut in, "They're smart enough to see a score lucrative enough to retire. It's not just the diamond. That's just the icing on the cake. That museum has a late-night exhibit, and they're the ones running security."

Chief Watanabe looked at the names; he looked at the security teams that had been in charge of the museums that had been set up so far. It was all there, and Arlo and he both knew it. It added up too perfectly not to be the truth. "So why do I need to meet your little group? I have the information you claim, saying I have dirty cops at my station. What's to stop me from arresting them right now?"

Arlo knew this question was coming. He needed to convince Watanabe to work with him now. "The information's convenient enough and interesting enough to look into, but not so much that we can stop." He pulled the puzzle apart with his old partner, "That's why I think it's The Chocolatier who gave me that info. I think he's planning to pave the streets the same night. I think he's planning something big, and I think he wants us distracted."

Watanabe sighed and stood again. This time, though, he didn't pause. He walked toward the exit.

Arlo hung his head as he realized the truth. He should've known the water was too murky to tread. Once trust was broken, he couldn't just put it back together again. But his bleak thoughts were interrupted as

Watanabe returned with his coat. "Come on. I'm not leaving my coat out of arm's length in a place like this."

Arlo smiled faintly at the unspoken truth of the matter. Watanabe had just agreed to work with his old partner. The two went to join the others.

Arlo started right into the heart of the matter when he sat down. "We all have different motives to be here. Sally, you're here because it's your diamond on the line. Rip, it's your neck in the noose. Chief, it's some bad apples in your precinct. Larry, Terry, and Jerry, it seems like you guys just like Toots and are willing to help out."

Larry began, "Exacta—"

Terry was the one to finish the word, "Mundo." Arlo just shook his head. He didn't like to work with amateurs.

Parker stepped in to smooth the process. "We have a lot of problems ahead of us."

Arlo couldn't help but think they were similar to the birds in a way as he finished Parker's thought. "And we're gonna come up with some solutions here."

Toots threw in a final sentiment for everyone at the table. "And we're all going to get along while we do that, right, you two?"

Arlo and Parker both rolled their eyes but nodded. Parker ruffled Arlo's head as he laid out the basic issue, "We have two crimes going down the same night."

Arlo added on to this, "Most likely at the same time."

McMack leaned forward and considered this. "That's going to take some serious coordination to stop both." Arlo was relieved that he wasn't dwelling on anything other than solutions. He took the premise of the issue at face value. He, at least, seemed to still trust Arlo that much despite their recent altercation.

Arlo tried to meet McMack's gaze, but McMack wouldn't match his. Toots jumped in with the next problem. "And what's worse, if the Chocolatier catches our scent ahead of time, he's back in his sewers and gone."

Arlo moved past his own problems with McMack to lay it out for everyone else. "Like McMack said, we need two teams in constant coordination. That way, neither criminal gets scent of us on their tail."

McMack nodded as he looked at the table. He mused aloud, "If the crooked cops catch scent, won't they just bail on the night? It's not just The Chocolatier we could lose. How do we have our force stationed and ready to go without notice?" Arlo nodded and thought about that problem as well.

Parker jumped in. "Those two teams will be separated into two teams of their own if this is going to work. Observers and engagers. Half the team will be in the shadows, and the other hiding in plain sight. It's the only way to ensure we have our bases covered without scaring off either target. A group that looks like they should be there, and a group that keeps an eye on both situations. Does that make sense?"

Parker looked around the table for confirmation. Watanabe pursed his lips and threw in another complication. "If this is going to work, I need our people." The Chief of Police paused to gesture to himself and McMack. "On every team. I don't trust everyone here."

The imposing man looked pointedly at Rip, sitting across from him.

Parker did his best to move through the awkwardness. "Fair enough."

Arlo joined his partner's attempt to push through. "So, coordination and timing are our first hurdle, but radios should help that."

Toots nodded but didn't agree as she said, "Except that we can't just have open communication when those rats could be behind any corner on lookout."

Arlo knew that was their biggest problem in the whole operation. Rats could be anywhere, listening in at any time. Still, Arlo decided to point out the positive. "We've got rats of our own, though. Just with wings." Larry, Jerry, and Terry each had looks of indignation on their faces at this, but none of them spoke against the declaration. Arlo knew why; they weren't here to help him, they were here to help Toots.

Watanabe stroked his chin as he tackled the first hurdle. "Timing is critical, so primary positions are crucial. One group in the museum, one out. One in the skies searching for the cul-de-sac that The Chocolatier hits, and one on the streets ready to move on target."

Rip threw in the additional hurdle nobody had mentioned yet. "We're talking so much about our own timing, but what if the timing of the actual culprits isn't as well timed as we hope? What if they move differently, and we have to prioritize which target to move on? It's all well and good for you all, but one of these targets is actively using me as a scapegoat! I need some assurance—"

McMack cut into Rip's increased agitation, "There's also the matter of mobilization. Timing is crucial, but it doesn't matter at all if we can't mobilize efficiently."

Sally joined in the conversation here, "Would it be helpful to use my twin sister?" The whole table paused at that question.

Parker licked his lips in consternation before posing the question, "Why would that be needed?"

Sally continued as though it were obvious, "In case I need a real gotcha moment with the criminal. Like they think they've abducted me, but it's my sister." She emphatically nodded as she spoke, and without noticing, she left the table somewhat speechless.

Parker looked down and back up a few times before questioning the obvious. "What?" His finger left his temple as he squinted his eyes, wondering what she meant.

McMack took the issue seriously; concern crept into his voice. "We're not letting anyone get abducted, right?"

Watanabe rudely dismissed the idea as a nuisance, "That doesn't even make any sense."

Sally seemed put out as she muttered, "I was just asking in case it helped…"

The table grew quiet as they had all been derailed. Arlo eventually voiced, "Anyway. There's a lot of hurdles."

Parker couldn't help but laugh as he added, "So, let's get to work." With that, Parker laid out a map of the city on the table, and the group began to come together to formulate a real plan.

Chapter 16
The Crows Sing at 8.53 p.m.

On a typical day, the city's largest museum looked impressive enough: the vast marble stairwell with imposing lions on either side, the large pillars leading to the entrance, and a massive architectural beauty that all supported one of the country's largest collections of art. At night, the museum was something out of a fairy tale. The night was dark with thick clouds above, and the wind was gently blowing. The museum had a red carpet with flashy lights, which illuminated and cast shadows across the landscape. Extravagantly dressed people and animals arrived in chauffeured cars and walked into the expo. The gentle breeze blew through the various heads and bodies of hair to create volume and glamor.

Arlo looked up in the sky, where he could just make out three crows flying overhead and away from the museum. He thought about the plan and wondered how long it would take everyone to get in position. The entire police force was lurking somewhere in the shadows, but his focus was on the sky. *The crows are our eyes in the sky*, he thought. *While the entire police force sits outside the museum and waits to move in on the dirty cops, The Chocolatier's gonna make their move. We need to know which street he's gonna hit. That's up to them. Team Red, Team Green, and Team Blue.*

A limo arrived, and Rip stepped out. He casually walked around the side of the limo and opened the door to let Sally out on the other side. Arlo continued placing the pieces in his mind: 'Rip and Sally are our eyes on the inside of the museum. It's her family's diamond, and he's the scape dog anyway. No one'll think twice about them being at the event. They're Team Deco.'

Arlo and Watanabe sat in darkness in Watanabe's car. They were at the farthest end of the museum's parking lot, watching. Both got out of the car and leaned against it. They watched the spectacle of the museum from the darkness. 'Watanabe and I are running the op at the museum. We're Team Diamond. Arlo placed the final pieces in his mind even as they received confirmation over their radios that everyone was ready to go: 'Toots, Parker, and McMack are running The Chocolatier op. They're Team Chocolate. We all have radios and earpieces, but that doesn't make me think this is going to go any easier than if we didn't. We assigned code names, and even took the city and broke it down into sectors for our investigation. That way, if a rat overhears us, they won't be able to make sense of it until it's too late. Still, it all feels too calm and collected. In a city of moving pieces and motivations, how can we be sure this'll go our way?'

Watanabe broke the silence with a hushed concern, "I don't like all my forces being on one target." This wasn't the first time the Police Chief had voiced concern that Arlo was the one trying to keep his forces on one target to let the other escape.

Arlo knew the man well. They'd worked together in the past. He wasn't concerned about his police force, just the three thieves. "It's not really your fault, you know. Those three? They made their decision, and—"

Watanabe cut in, "Traitors know traitors, I suppose." Arlo took a deep breath to try not to rise to the bait. "They're thieves. That's all there is to it."

Arlo couldn't coddle the man anymore. He criticized, "Just think of it like this: all your eyes are on Rip right now. Isn't that how you've had your forces spread lately anyway?" Watanabe merely frowned before Arlo shrugged. "I tried my best."

Toots and Parker sat in the front seat of Parker's car. McMack sat in the back seat while he anxiously chewed a bone. Parker looked into the back seat at McMack's chewing and said, "Ya know. Arlo does that when he's stressed out too." His face turned to concern at the dog's stress. "You all right back there?"

McMack's reply was muffled by the bone. "Mmm'll be metter once moonlight's over."

Toots turned back to the German Shepherd and winked. "You don't like our company?"

McMack stopped chewing this time to reply, "I think Arlo's beginning to rub off on you, Toots."

Toots beamed at this. Parker smiled at her, beaming and voiced the obvious, "I'm not sure he meant that as a compliment."

Toots just kept on smiling. She replied to them both, "I guess it's up to me whether I take it as one or not. Not up to him and his intent."

Parker laughed while McMack went back to his anxious chewing. "Still," Parker said, "I get what you mean. It's pretty nerve-wracking just waiting for word from some birds about the case of the year." Parker picked up the radio in the car and played with the buttons to make sure it was still working. "Red Team? Can you read?"

Larry's voice cawed back from the radio, "I read you loud and clear, Team Chocolate."

Parker nodded in satisfaction that everything still worked. He put the radio back down for just a moment before he picked it back up.

Toots gave the human a look as she cut through to his real concern, "Arlo's gonna be fine, too."

Parker looked at her, and the concern was easily visible on his face. He confided his concern thanks to the prompting from the small dog. "Since I've known him, we work cases together. It's been a weird couple of weeks."

"He's with the Chief of Police," Toots soothed. "What could go wrong?"

McMack scoffed at that and muttered from the back seat, "Wouldn't surprise me if that *is* the problem for them both. Those two..." He trailed off thanks to a glare from Toots and apologized, "Sorry."

McMack went back to focusing on his bone, and Toots tried to change the topic, "I'm more worried the rats are gonna overhear something and tip him off."

Parker nodded. "Me too, but everything's in motion now. Tonight either goes well or it doesn't." He sighed heavily, and his fingers wrapped around the steering wheel.

McMack chose to abandon the bone this time. He threw it on the floor of the car and put his head forward between the other two. "So, let's make sure our part goes well."

The radio came alive as Larry's voice came through. "Checking in, I have a potential spot in sector 6."

Parker turned the car on and began driving as Toots looked at the map of the city to direct him to what they had defined as sector 6. As they drove, Terry's voice came through this time, "I thought I was in sector 6."

These birds weren't professionals by any means. On the open channel, they debated each other; Larry replied, "You're in sector 5."

Parker stopped the car at what Terry said next, "Oh. Potential sighting in sector 5 then too."

Jerry's voice excitedly rang through next, "Guys. Sector 7 too!"

McMack leaned over Toots' shoulder to look at the map. Concern grew on his face before he took the radio and replied to the birds, "OK. Team Red go to the next sector. Team Blue and Green stay on current targets."

Parker started driving again. He looked at McMack to confirm what he thought the dog was doing. "We go check out sector 6 to confirm while they keep up patrol."

"I have a bad feeling about this." McMack replied. Parker just drove silently into the wintery night of the city.

Arlo and Watanabe hadn't moved, but the scene outside the museum had completely died down. All the action had moved inside. Arlo laughed while he thought about Sally and Rip working together. "How do you think those two are getting on?"

Watanabe replied flatly, "Weird pair, if ever there was one."

Arlo nodded and gripped their radio tightly. He thought to himself that the entire crew was a pretty unlikely group to work together.

Inside the museum, the main room of the event had the diamond as the centerpiece. There were Roman statues and busts standing amidst the mingling crowd, and the museum's best paintings had been moved to line the walls of this singular room. The ball was glamorous and expensive. There was catering, people drinking from fancy glasses, and food being carried around on trays to the most wealthy and influential people in the city. Sally and Rip laughed obnoxiously with a fancy-looking pair that excused themselves. Rip's laugh died down in an instant when he stopped acting. "This suit's so stuffy."

Sally petted the dog on his head and tried to calm the rough around the edges Pitbull down. "You're doing great." Rip sneered and growled at Sally's words and hand. She pulled her gloved hand back and asked him condescendingly, "Would you prefer I say 'Good Dog?'"

Rip rolled his eyes. "I'll just be happy when this—" He abruptly cut short when he spotted a commotion across the room. "That's not normal at this sort of event, is it?"

Sally looked at what Rip pointed to. Someone was making a complete fool of themselves. They knocked from statue to bust. They almost knocked over multiple artifacts. A security guard grabbed the man by his arms and dragged him off.

Sally just sighed. "Unfortunately, at these events, it can happen." She touched her earpiece just briefly to open communication with Arlo and Chief Watanabe. "Team Deco checking in. We have a problem."

Rip and Sally could both hear Watanabe in their ears. "Team Diamond, I hear you."

Sally tried to keep anyone around them from hearing her as she replied, "Someone's making a fool of themselves. I'm worried they're going to call the police to come pick this guy up."

Watanabe sounded irritated with his response, "What's the problem?"

Rip shook his head, gritted his teeth, and spoke into his own radio, "Won't your boys in blue arriving scare off the thieves?"

Watanabe's smirk could practically be heard when he questioned Rip, "Would it stop you? If you were in their position? One squad car shows up and takes away some idiot. Your whole plan's up in smoke." Rip took a deep breath, and Sally let out a sigh of relief. Watanabe continued, "Just keep cool, you two. Don't create problems because you're nervous. I've got a squad car ready to—"

Rip interrupted the Chief, "I read you. Hold onto it for twelve minutes."

Watanabe's pompous attitude dropped at this. "Twelve minutes? We want to get this over—"

Rip didn't give the man any semblance of respect. He cut him off again. "That's how long it takes typical response time in this area," he said this as though it were common knowledge.

Watanabe clicked his tongue. "Copy." Then, he clicked off the radio communication from his end.

Sally raised an eyebrow at the Pitbull in a suit. "That's how long the typical response time takes?"

Rip shrugged and gave a toothy grin. "I'm a fountain of knowledge with fun facts."

Sally laughed and snagged two shrimp balls being carried by them. She handed one to Rip. "I would normally love a gala like this," she said to fill the empty space between them as they both ate. "What do you think their 'go' will be? Will there be a signal? When do the others show up?"

Rip nodded toward their single target. The police officer moonlighting tonight stood by an exit to the room. He hadn't moved since they walked in. "That's the question." Rip gestured to the other security guards, "There's three security guards in the front. One to each side."

Sally finished the count. "And two across the room. I know, but—"

Rip shrugged now and confirmed her doubts about the situation. "All we can do is keep an eye on them. We know that one's involved, but any of the others could be too."

Sally smiled as she grabbed a drink being carried by. "So, let's try to enjoy ourselves?"

Rip smiled, despite himself. "I guess we can do that too."

McMack and Parker arrived at the street Larry had sent them to. They saw a small paving machine actively working its way up the dark street, with a silhouetted figure driving it cautiously. Parker shrugged and looked at the other two. "Looks like we got the right one. Let's move in?"

Toots frowned and held out a paw. "Hang on. McMack, do you have binoculars?"

McMack placed a pair of binoculars into her hands without hesitation. "Night vision and everything. Top of the line."

Toots looked through them and held them above her snout as she commanded, "Get the birds on the radio."

McMack immediately clicked the radio on but waited to speak into it. "What's wrong?"

Parker seemed to realize what she was getting at before being told, as he exclaimed quietly, "Oh, no!"

McMack shook his head, but the birds checked in. He leaned back and asked each one for status updates.

Toots never looked away from the binoculars. She and Parker talked over the status updates in the back seat. "Exactly."

It seemed the status update was just a formality for Parker and Toots. Parker asked Toots, "Who is it then? If it isn't him?"

McMack sighed heavily and confirmed the other two's suspicions. "Team Green says it's The Chocolatier in sector 5. Blue says sector 6 as well. The paving's begun there too. Team Red has already spotted him in sector 8. What do you see, Toots? How can he be multiple places at once?"

Toots handed the German Shepherd the binoculars as she gave him the answer, "It's the rats. He taught the rats how to do it. Those were all practice runs. They're paving the whole city tonight."

Parker clenched a fist in frustration. "We have to find which one is him."

McMack put the binoculars back down and furthered the problem, "Without scaring him back into the sewers." He sighed and pulled the radio back to his face. He changed the channel on it to "Team Diamond." He was calling Arlo and Watanabe now, "Team Diamond, Team Chocolate checking in."

Watanabe had taken a phone call in the car while Arlo kept watch outside. The man joined the small dog to watch the museum again. "That was dispatch," Watanabe explained, "the three other suspects just volunteered to pick up this guy from the museum."

Arlo nodded with a furrowed brow as they worked through the art thieves' plan. "So, it's their plan. Security brings this guy to some holding room until the police show up; they act like they're picking him up, but instead—"

Watanabe sighed and looked at the ground. "They get the art." He shook his head and vented, "Part of me was still holding out hope you were wrong or that you were the bad dog here all along."

Arlo laughed at the disappointed man. "Same here. I was wrong anyway."

The two waited and watched while the police car arrived in much less time than twelve minutes. They watched it park around the side of the museum. The officers in the car didn't make any move to get out of the car. Watanabe pulled out the police-issued binoculars and looked at the suspects. "It's them, all right. Here. Look."

Arlo took a look himself. Three officers sat in the car, all dressed in black. "Those are our guys." Arlo wondered for a moment longer. 'What were they waiting for?'

Inside the museum, Rip and Sally stood in a group of seven or eight individuals. They laughed and engaged in conversation as best they could while keeping an eye on the security guards. The two blended in seamlessly. Sally whispered to Rip discreetly, "When are they gonna make their move already?"

Rip replied out of the side of his mouth, "I don't know. But we have a problem." He pointed out the window in front of the pair, and Sally followed along the line of sight. On the rooftop of a neighboring building, the two could clearly see one of the police lookouts.

Sally immediately called in to the two running the show, "Team Diamond., Team Deco checking in. We have another problem."

Watanabe sounded exasperated. "Team Deco. The suspects are on sight. What's wrong?"

Sally urgently whispered while she turned away from the group she and Rip stood among, "We can clearly see one of the lookouts."

Watanabe challenged them yet again, "So what?"

Rip growled in frustration, startling one of the others in the group. The startled person jumped and held their hand to their chest as they laughed it off with concern on their face. Rip ignored them and whispered the obvious, "So, if we can. They can, too. And you bet they're looking for that kind of thing more than us."

Watanabe let his hand holding the radio fall glumly before picking it back up and changing the channel on it. He licked his lips in irritation and passed the message along to the team on lookout. "Lookout. You've been spotted. Get out and be ready to move in." Then the man turned to Arlo. "We might have to move early."

Arlo shook his head. "We don't have the evidence."

Watanabe started to reply, "I know, but—" However, he was interrupted by the radio again. This time it was Team Chocolate checking in.

McMack's voice called through with concern, "Team Diamond. Team Diamond. Team Chocolate checking in."

Arlo took the radio from the fuming Police Chief. "Team Diamond. I read you."

McMack's voice was flat and straight to the point. "We have a problem."

Arlo put his paw on his face. He felt his own frustration mounting, just like Watanabe's. "Oh, great. So do we," he replied, "what's yours?"

Chapter 17
Stretching's Important for a Flexible Plan

Team Chocolate drove as quickly as they could through the streets to check the next 'Chocolatier.' Luckily, McMack was with Parker and Toots, so they had a police siren in the car to ensure they moved safely through the streets.

McMack was practically yelling into the radio when he and Arlo finished relaying the various problems that had arisen. "You need to stall until we find the real one!" McMack hung up the radio and looked forward in anticipation.

"What if—" Toots started but paused uncertainly.

McMack was more curt than usual. "What?"

Parker proved to be on the same wavelength as Toots yet again. "She's worried that the Chocolatier isn't out tonight at all. That he's in his sewers, letting his rats do all the work."

McMack leaned forward in his seat and nodded in understanding. Then he shook his head after a moment of thought. "No. No, my gut tells me he wouldn't do that."

Toots looked at the dog, whose head was about the size of her entire body. "Why not?"

"He's targeting streets where exterminators have been, right?" McMack answered with a rhetorical question. "He's doing this for them because they've been getting poisoned. He wouldn't put them in danger without putting himself in the mix too. I have to believe that. I have to hope that." He seemed to be trying to convince himself more than Toots.

Parker moved the conversation on to more practical matters. "How long can they stall? Did they say?"

McMack sighed in response. Toots turned off the siren herself and pointed down a side street. "There!" she shouted. "Stop!" Parker took the car slowly down that street and stopped the engine short of where the cul-de-sac in question was. Toots looked through the night-vision goggles and disappointedly put them back down. "No. More rats."

The car immediately began driving to the next place, and the crows called out. They moved on to the next one with no way of knowing if the next would prove more fruitful than the last.

Arlo and Watanabe were pacing. "It's gonna take better timing." Arlo worked through the problems for the fifth or sixth time at this point. "But let's tip off the reporter about The Chocolatier." That was a new solution for the two.

Watanabe stopped pacing and looked at the car in the distance. "That's a major risk, Arlo. They need us to stall right now."

Arlo nodded, and his lip got stuck on his tooth. He frowned. "As soon as we have a street, we call Lin, and we move."

"What if they leave?" Watanabe countered. "Before that happens?"

The timing was falling apart around them as one crime was underway, with no way of knowing where the head of the proverbial snake was. The other crime hadn't even really begun. Arlo considered their options and problems before proposing a gamble, "Then give them something fake?"

The chief of police wasn't big on gambling. "That's an even bigger risk. We could lose both targets."

"What choice do we have?" Arlo did his best to keep his voice down. "We need them to believe we've gotten out of here, or they won't move and we have nothing!"

"Fine," Watanabe relented. "The second we have confirmation of The Chocolatier spotting." He then spoke into the radio, "Team Chocolate. We need photo evidence of The Chocolatier in case he gets away. We're putting it all on the line here." Wearily, the man slumped into the front seat of his car. The two had just committed to a new plan. They were going to bluff the thieves, potentially alert The Chocolatier, and involve the press, which could end up making them look like complete fools to the public.

Parker was moving on from another bust as the radio chimed in with Jerry's voice, "I have a sighting! It's different! The driver looks bigger."

The three were pretty down and out when they understood what Arlo and Watanabe's new plan meant for them. If they didn't find The Chocolatier soon, he'd disappear without a single photo of proof, let alone catching the man. If the press were involved before an arrest was made, it also meant the chance of catching them failing on camera, which wouldn't be good for Arlonius Investigation's business. "Where?" McMack urgently asked, "Where?"

Jerry cawed back in response, "Sector 15!"

Toots had been studying the map the entire time they'd been driving from street to street. She didn't even look at it when she directed Parker, "That's 8th and Mission!"

Parker looked at the dog with concern. She hadn't called out destinations like that without review to this point. "You sure?" he asked. "Look at the map to—"

Toots barked back and put the siren back on. "I'm sure!"

Parker set off in a different direction. If she took time to look at the map, they would've missed a shorter route through the highway. Luckily, they hit the highway hard and went fast towards their new destination. McMack switched the radio away from the birds and called into it, "Team Diamond. Team Diamond! 8th and Mission. We have the street, and we're moving there now."

Arlo sucked in air and nodded to Watanabe. The Chief took out his cell phone and called the reporter, Lin. "Hi Lin. Yes, yes. I know." He was having trouble getting a word in with the reporter as she made pleasantries. "Listen." He cut in finally, "I need you to get down to 8th and Mission St. We're in hot pursuit of The Chocolatier right now. I know you've been reporting on this case so far, and I want you to be the one who gets on the scene first. Yeah. You owe me one." Watanabe sighed, hung up, and took the binoculars out to look at the art thieves in the police car.

Arlo nudged the man gently. "Call dispatch and get all units to move there." He said this as though he were speaking to a child who might throw a tantrum.

Watanabe was cautious as ever. "Might be laying it on thick."

Arlo nodded but pressed, "It'd be more suspicious if they hear from the reporter that you guys are in hot pursuit than if they hear from dispatch that they're supposed to be there too." Watanabe shook his head, but they both knew Arlo was right. He went into the car to have dispatch reach out to all available units.

Parker, Toots, and McMack arrived and slowed the car to a crawl before they parked with The Chocolatier barely in view. They got out on the far side of the car to prep their roles in this next act of their grand plan. Parker handed out the cameras. He whispered, "Take these. If he runs, Toots. Let him. He's tried to hurt someone before you can't—"

Toots took the camera and ignored the rest. She took off to go get the shot of The Chocolatier that would put him away. She moved with determination and left Parker and McMack in partial disbelief at the small dog's tenacity. Parker and McMack shrugged at each other before McMack took off the other direction. Parker used the largest camera and immediately stood it on the hood of the car. He started taking pictures right away. It wasn't the best angle, but it was something if the others couldn't get shots in time. Parker whispered encouragement to himself, "We need *something* outta this."

Toots made her way closer and closer. Periodically, she stopped to take pictures. Then she moved on to try to get closer and closer. She also tried to encourage herself by whispering to herself through the adrenaline, "Okay. Steady. Shoot. Move closer. Repeat. You're bred to hunt, girl. You're bred to hunt."

Arlo and Watanabe watched silently with baited breath. Finally, the doors opened to the police car. The three men in black made their way silently to the back door of the museum. Arlo looked at Watanabe and nodded before they both crept closer. A light snowfall began as the two figures made their way towards the art thieves. All the pieces were in motion. All that mattered now was catching both parties and not letting anyone get away.

Sally and Rip continued to act nonchalant while they purveyed the scene of the museum. Rip spotted one of the security guards holding his ear before exiting the room. The Pitbull looked at Sally knowingly, and she spotted it too. "I'm going after him." Rip surprised Sally with this announcement.

"No, we just call in that they're on the move. What do you mean?" she asked.

Rip was already moving towards the door. He answered back, "I'm not letting him come back through here. I'm gonna surround him." Rip took off through the doorway after the guard. Sally sighed, put down her drink, and followed. The plan had gone sideways, but everyone was making moves to make it work anyway.

Arlo and Watanabe had moved alongside the thieves getaway car opposite the museum. They used it for cover while Watanabe whispered into his radio, "Move in. Support Team Chocolate and get in position for Team Diamond." There was no going back now, as teams were in full throttle. Figures suddenly appeared in all corners of the parking lot. They moved in and joined Watanabe and Arlo in surrounding the unsuspecting art thieves. The snow was coming down a little heavier now around the figures moving through the night. Dozens of sets of footprints appeared and disappeared as everyone got in position.

Toots and McMack now had The Chocolatier surrounded and were taking pictures from every angle. The snow had reached here as well and made it difficult to get a good shot. They were dangerously close in order to get anything resembling a picture of The Chocolatier. A rat scurried through the snow and up to the hot chocolate steaming at the beginning of the storm. The rat went up to The Chocolatier, and Toots took a picture of the two conversing. She was certain she got his face in that one. It was over for The Chocolatier.

The Chocolatier moved with surprising agility. He abandoned his paving machine and ran towards a manhole. McMack broke his cover and shouted after the fleeing man, "Freeze!" The Mole Man did no such thing. Toots watched from behind a bush while McMack ran the man down and prepared to launch at him. A moment later, the sirens could be heard, and they knew why he'd run. The police were almost here. Chaos broke out. Toots put her head down in fear. A figure streaked past her, and she watched where Parker went into action to assist McMack.

Toots steeled her nerves and urged herself to follow. "You signed up for this. *Ugh,*" she grunted with dismay at herself and took off after Parker and McMack towards the culprit.

McMack tackled The Chocolatier and tried to pin the man. However, the man quickly scooped some melted chocolate and tried to push it into the dog's mouth. Parker arrived moments later and pinned the man's arm, which was full of chocolate. The Chocolatier didn't stop struggling as he clenched his fist to punch Parker. Toots arrived this time and bit the man's wrist. She tasted iron while she held the man's second arm with her jaws.

The three each slowed their breathing while they waited for backup to arrive. The snow was coming down thickly around the four figures, whose struggle had become a muted, silent effort of endurance. The sirens grew louder. McMack reprimanded the other two, "You're both civilians. You shouldn't have—"

Parker flatly interrupted, "I don't care." They all paused, and the adrenaline died down. Parker turned to Toots and said, "I told you to—"

Toots flatly interrupted, "I don't care." It started as a chuckle from McMack, but soon all three laughed and expelled every ounce of relief aloud. Their backup arrived to find the three laughing uproariously over a struggling man letting out guttural screeches and cries for help into the stormy night.

Watanabe and Arlo lead a team of police to the back door of the museum. From the shadows, they watched while art was handed from the security guard and a supposed fool getting arrested to the three officers dressed in black. They had what they needed. Watanabe motioned for everyone to go. He led the way and shouted out, "Freeze!" The thieves took off running immediately. The officers had all but surrounded the thieves. Still, two managed to find holes and escape. Arlo ran after one that headed away from the museum and towards the park. The other ran back inside the museum. Arlo chased the man into the park, snapping at his heels all the while.

The man cried out when Arlo finally got a hold of his leg and dragged him down. They came down together atop a thin layer of snow. The man grasped at his leg and stopped struggling due to the damage Arlo had done to him. The snow was strewn about, brown and red, and showed their path all the way back to the museum.

Arlo took in the park and realized he was at the foot of the tree where Toots had buried her collar. Arlo smiled and sat on the crying man's back. He waited until Watanabe arrived on the scene. Arlo got up, and the man rose slowly with his hands raised. Arlo could feel a blast from the past when Watanabe sounded like he had when they'd been partners. "Good job, Arlo. Good dog."

With a smirk of satisfaction, Watanabe slapped the handcuffs on the art thief. The Chief of Police and the private investigator walked the limping man back to the museum together.

When they took the man towards the police van to join his buddies in the back, the man tried to plead. His voice was filled with panic. "You can't be serious, Chief. We're doing this city a favor! That dog, Rip! He doesn't deserve to walk free! So, what if we get paid for the work we do? We're owed it, aren't we? We put our lives on the line, and that guy just gets out on a technicality any time we bring him in! Let's just call this what it is; it isn't too late to do the right thing."

Surprisingly, Watanabe paused at the entrance of the van. Arlo couldn't help but wonder which would win out: Watanabe's incredibly narrow-minded sense of justice or his desire to get criminals off the street? Watanabe finally broke the silence quietly. "I do my job. You should've done yours." With that, he threw the man into the van and closed the door behind him.

"You know." Arlo said, "For a second, I wondered if you were tempted."

Watanabe looked away in what Arlo could only assume was a sense of shame. "I was, and that scares me. I thought you and I were different, but here I am—"

Arlo sighed and interrupted the melodrama, "We got the guys, partner."

Watanabe touched his hand to his face and laughed. "It wasn't so bad working together again."

Arlo wasn't sure he'd go that far. "Maybe," he replied.

Watanabe sounded hopeful. "Maybe we'll work together again." Arlo wondered if this was wishful thinking. The two had been partners before, sure, but things had changed since then.

Arlo decided to dismiss this as jovially as he could. "Hope not, Chief. A lot of bad things had to happen to bring us together this time."

Watanabe chuckled, and the two looked around at some commotion coming their way. Sally and Rip both exited the museum, pushing a bruised and battered art thief in front of them. Sally called out ahead, "Hey! We got one too!" Sally waved while she brought the perp forward with Rip. Rip just chuckled at her enthusiasm. Arlo and Watanabe looked at each other in surprise before waving back to Sally. They didn't wait for the last thief to be put in the van before they returned to Watanabe's car and drove to the other crime scene.

Arlo and Watanabe drove up to the street and found it was half paved in chocolate. Parker, Toots, and McMack were already giving an interview to the reporter, Lin. They did arrive in time to see The Chocolatier being put into a police car. As he was pushed into the car, he shouted out, "Keep filthy poison off streets if you want me no poison your dogs! Rats no ask for this! We not ask for this! Filthy uppers! Filthy city!" The reporter had stopped the interview long enough to get the exclamations from the man before his head was finally pushed into the car.

Arlo thought for a moment, but he had to know. He called out to the officer who'd closed the door, "Hang on a second." Trotting over, he tapped the window. "I got one question for him." The officer looked confused for a moment, but Watanabe came over and nodded his approval. The officer went to the front and cracked the window. Inside, The Chocolatier was still fuming and yelling. Arlo waited until he stopped to ask his question, "Is it us? Did dogs do something to you? I don't get it. I get the exterminator. You're mad about your rats, but…"

The Mole Man's ire seemed to wane for just a moment as he looked Arlo in the eyes. The two had a connection that made Arlo uncomfortable. They'd both used each other up to this point, and it had been an odd game of chess maneuvering each other to 'clean the streets.' Mole Man calmed enough to reply in the face of his adversary, "Nothin'. Dogs do nothin' wrong by me. Uppers, though. They come for my rats first. Eye for eye." He looked away from Arlo as he repeated, "Eye for eye."

The scene calmed, the interview resumed, and Watanabe and Arlo watched from the side as the three representatives gave their take on the chocolatier case. They notably left out any information involving the art thieves being part of the case.

Watanabe didn't look at Arlo when he said, "You could take it public. This whole thing. Every bit of it's going down in my report, anyway. Public knowledge will have it anyway. Arlonius Investigations solves two major crimes in one night."

Arlo didn't look at the man either. Instead, he watched his partner, Parker. He had thought about making a big deal about both cases, so the media came after Watanabe. "Yeah," he replied, "let's let the news cycle focus on the win here, though. We caught The Chocolatier. That's a high-profile case enough for Arlonius Investigations."

Watanabe didn't let it drop. "Any other time, a takedown of some crooked officers could get me fired. You'd be well within your rights to—"

Arlo interrupted, "Chief. Let's just enjoy the win." The two leaned back against the car until the others finished with the reporter and came up to them excitedly.

On the way over, Parker looked at his phone and held it up, waving. "Sally, Larry, Terry, and Jerry are already there. Anyone wants a round at Ruff's to celebrate?" Parker took the whole group's temperature on the idea.

Watanabe declined, "You'll have to forgive me, but I never want to go back to that seedy bar again."

Parker shrugged and asked McMack, "Your loss! McMack?"

McMack laughed and nodded. "Why not. Chief, think about coming along!"

The group jovially walked away, but Arlo couldn't help but get in one more word. "Besides. It never hurts to have The Chief of Police owe you a favor, right?" He cheekily winked at the frowning Chief of Police. Parker picked up and swung Arlo side to side in his arms like a baby while the group walked to his car. Arlo, like any good dog, hated the action but loved the attention from his favorite person. "I love this! I hate this! I love this! I hate this!"

Parker put Arlo down and hugged him. "Love you, pal."

Arlo, ever the stoic, looked away as he replied, "You too, partner." Though, he couldn't help but wag his tail enthusiastically.

Toots jumped between the two and reclaimed her spot as part of Arlonius Investigations, "Partners!"

Arlo laughed and confirmed, "Partners." Still feeling bad for biting McMack earlier, Arlo bumped into the big dog playfully. McMack smiled and bumped back. The four got in the car with Toots and McMack in the back seat, assuming Arlo would get shotgun. The persistent dog wasn't to be deterred this time, however, so he lay down in Parker's lap while the man laughed and drove towards Ruff's with the passenger seat empty.

Arlo considered what this case had done for him. How far he and his friends had come on a stale case that nobody could solve. How the media would follow this story only so long enough for something more exciting to show up in a day or two somewhere else in the city. How the snow that was falling had already removed any trace of the events of the night. The city would move forward, the people would forget, and Arlonius Investigations would get a few more cases in the next few months. Arlo thought, *Maybe I don't need to look behind me with friends at my side who have my back. Time to be like the city. Time to move forward. The past's in the past, and I can trust it'll stay there.*

Look out for book 2 – PI Arlo and the Case of Amnesia

www.ingramcontent.com/pod-product-compliance
Lightning Source LLC
Chambersburg PA
CBHW031001210726
48290CB00007B/2419